MW00911403

the ADVENTURES of BOONE

ALL ABOUT ME... AT FIRST

DAVID ELLIS

ILLUSTRATED BY NATE CHRISTENSON

The Adventures of Boone
All About Me...At First

Copyright © 2021 by David Ellis

ISBN: 978-0-9981476-9-7

Fergus Falls, MN 56537

First printing November 2021

All rights reserved. No part of this book may be reproduced in any form without written permission from the author, except for briefs excerpts in a review.

Format/Design by Minion Editing & Design   www.joyminion.com

Illustrations/Cover Design by Nate Christenson

Published by J.O.Y. Publishing

Printed in the United States of America

Order from:

David Ellis
davidwalterellis@gmail.com

Also available at:

Lundeen's (Fergus Falls, MN)
https://victorlundeens.com/

There would be no dedication page for this story without our grandchildren. They helped to write it. As we spent time together outside, their experiences and adventures in creation provided the ideas for *The Adventures of Boone – All About Me... At First*. Each chapter is formed around an actual experience that really happened outside. Most of these experiences are from time spent with grandchildren. There are also a significant number of chapters in *All About Me...At First* that are based on real life experiences I had alone or with others while outside. I really spearfish with a pastor.

This book is written to give God glory. There would not be a dedication page for this story without His creation. God's creation formed the backdrop for every chapter in this book. It is my prayer that as you read about the adventures of Boone, you will be drawn into your own experience with nature. Go outside like Boone. You really can see the divine nature and eternal power of God with every trip you take outside. May the will of God be done and His kingdom come in your life as you read *The Adventures of Boone – All About Me...At First*.

David W. Gaus
Romans 1:20

Contents

Scripture Readings

My prayer for you is that these verses from Scripture will lead you. There is one verse for each chapter. I suggest you read the verse before you begin the chapter...or if not, read it sometime while you are interacting with the book.

Chapter 1   *Romans 1:20*

Chapter 2   *Psalm 33:8-9*

Chapter 3   *Job 38:12-13*

Chapter 4   *Psalm 33*

Chapter 5   *Psalm 145:7*

Chapter 6   *Proverbs 17:17*

Chapter 7   *Luke 6:48*

Chapter 8   *Mark 4:39*

Chapter 9   *Exodus 20:12*

Chapter 10   *Psalm 145:5*

Chapter 11   *Ephesians 3:20*

Chapter 12   *Proverbs 27:17*

Chapter 13   *Proverbs 3:5-6*

Chapter 14   *Matthew 19:19*

Chapter 15   *Jeremiah 10:13*

Chapter 16   *Psalm 31:19*

Chapter 17   *Psalm 121:1-2*

Prologue

Why God's Word is in this Book

In the Bible, we find absolute truth. Every word, each chapter, all of the 66 books contained in the Bible are the Word of God. There is no book on earth like it. No book in the past, present or future is equal to it. No other book is the Word of God. And God does not lie. God knows all things. God has all power, and this should not surprise us; God is everywhere present...at once. Perhaps this should have been put in this paragraph first: God is real. God exists. This fact has an impact on all of life...every day, every minute, every second of human existence. God is in control of it all. This means what God says is important and carries weight – for eternity. He has given His Word to us to speak with us.

God's Word is the main influence in shaping Boone's character. It guides his parents and grandparents as they teach and instruct Boone. God's Word directly leads Boone. As we follow Boone through this period in his life, the influence of the Bible on Boone's life is clear.

All About Me...At First is a story of how God leads us and teaches us – through His Word, the Bible. While this is a story, God's Word works on real people's lives just as it did on Boone's. Boys and girls, dads and moms, grandpas and grandmas are touched by God when they read the Bible.

Please, enjoy the story of Boone! While you do, read God's Word. Come away with a change in your own life. For life is not "all about ME," as Boone discovered. This is God's world...real life is found in Him. As we read the Bible, we discover He loves you and me.

Author's Intro

The Adventures of Boone:
All About Me...At First

This is something new for me. It's been on my mind for an extraordinarily long time. Meet Boone. At the start of this account, he's an 11-year-old boy. He delights in the mysteries and wonders of nature. Creating Boone is my way to share with you my nature experiences. *Boone* means *good, a blessing.* His experiences are based on real events in nature. Almost all were experienced by me, or me with family. With the exception of Boone's fall through the ice, my eyes have seen what you will read about in this story. With eyes and heart, I have searched for the power and divine nature of God in each trip outside. These real experiences are the basis for Boone's story.

Growing up with normal stubborn behavior and disobedience, Boone needs help – he needs a "rescue." He needs time outside, where the power of God clearly can be seen. With guidance from his parents, Boone begins to find his own "power checks." As he spends time outside, he is taught to look for the power and divine nature of God. It can be found by anyone who spends time outside. Boone found it and it changed his life.

Perhaps this book will encourage you to seek your own power checks. When you do, you will find God every time. Enjoy this first adventure of Boone.

Introduction

Near Disaster

First ice had become one of Boone's favorite times of the year. He couldn't exactly explain why. Perhaps it was walking on a hard surface. That surface was liquid water in his warm water memories. Perhaps it was seeing an underwater world through clear ice. He found pleasure in exploring the frozen surface of a lake before snow covered the artistry of fresh ice. It was always beautiful. He was sure that a chance to go fishing was part of first ice thrills. But there was also another reason. If you asked him, he would admit that the hint of danger added to the thrill.

He was on first ice now, his grandfather behind him pulling the portable fish house and their gear. Boone was leading. With an ice chisel in his hand, it was his job to continually check for ice depth. It was actually easy. With every other step Boone raised the chisel and plunged it iceward. If his downward and forceful stroke did not plunge the chisel through the ice, it was safe to walk on. But...if it plunged through...it was a sign to stop immediately. The next step was to move backward, carefully, away from the dangerous thin ice.

As they walked, with Boone checking the ice and Grandpa pulling the fish house, Grandpa reminded Boone to slide his hand through the loop in the chisel rope. "That way you'll not lose the chisel if it breaks through. And Boone, if something unexpected happens and you find yourself breaking through the ice, flip the chisel to horizontal. It may be enough to hold you up and keep you from going under."

Boone's "yes" answer did not reveal his thoughts about breaking through the ice. He was frightened by the thought of it, but his pride did not allow him to say that to his grandfather. With the heavy clothes and boots he was wearing, he was sure he would sink like a rock. *Oh, it would be so cold*, he thought.

As Boone looked at the ice they walked on, he could see cracks from top to bottom of the ice sheet. The ice cracked from expanding and contracting, but was still solid.

As if he could understand Boone's thoughts, his grandpa said, "Boone, the cracks look about five or six inches deep. We are on ice safe for walking." Boone thought so too.

It happened while they were talking about the beautiful ice patterns formed from a warm day yesterday. Where the thin coat of snow on the ice had melted, there were patches of ice needles. They were black and raised from the surface of the rest of the ice. His grandpa pointed them out first. Once Boone was aware of them, he was fascinated by them. Thinking back, Boone thought that was the reason he stopped plunging the chisel down to check the ice. He just kept walking looking for ice needles.

He had no warning. There was a slight cracking sound, then Boone felt himself falling into the water. He tried flipping the chisel horizontal.

For a moment the chisel held him up. His boots filled with icy water. He felt the frigid water soak his socks.

A second crack occurred just before Boone's head went underwater. The freezing shock of the cold water made him gasp. He had enough sense to not open his mouth and gulp in the cold water. Then he felt himself sinking.

His split-second response was not fear – he realized he had to shake off the chisel or he would never be able to swim back to the surface. His water-soaked mitten came off with the chisel. He tried to kick to the surface. His water-soaked boots held him back. His lungs were desperate for a breath by now. Then he felt his feet touch bottom. He could not remember how he got his boots off, only that he pushed up from the bottom in a desperate motion to get back to the surface – and air.

When his head broke the surface, he heard a loud gasp – and realized it was his own. He went under again, but this time not far. He remembered that he knew how to tread water. As he held his arms out and circle paddled, he slowly kicked his feet. His head came above the water again...and stayed there as he continued to swim in place. By now he realized how sharp and piercing the cold water was. He knew he would not stay up much longer, already his arms and legs felt too heavy to move.

Then he saw a rope sailing over him. It landed exactly over his head. How? Where?

He heard Grandpa say, "Put it under your arms."

With great difficulty and ever-stiffening arms, Boone did it. He felt himself bump against the edge of the ice. He heard a shout: "KICK! KICK!" Boone kicked his remaining strength. Then he was sliding on safe ice.

He saw his grandpa backing quickly away from the death hole in the ice. Just as quickly, his grandpa had the sled next to him. In one motion he rolled Boone on top of the sled and the equipment. Boone remembered saying in a shivering voice, "Grandpa, what about the chisel?"

All he remembered hearing was, "We'll get another one. You're freezing!"

He may have passed out from hypothermia. He could not remember how he came to be sitting in a warm pickup. Then he remembered why his clothes were soaked. He felt his grandfather's hand on his shoulder.

"Boone, you and I just experienced one of God's marvelous miracles. When we left the shore, I saw that rope in the storage bin in the pickup door. I thought, why take this with us? My next thought was, oh, I need to. I laid it at the front of the fish house sled.

When you broke through, I bent down and grabbed it. When you bobbed up the first time, I tied the loop and coiled the rope to throw. I've never thrown a lasso before. Imagine how stunned I was when I saw the rope settle over your head!

I thought the ice would break as I pulled you up, or that your clothes would catch on a sharp edge. But you slid out smooth and easy. I could have shouted, 'Thanks be to God!' then, but you needed to get warmed up fast. I ran you back as fast as my nearly 70-year-old legs could move.

Here we are, both safe. We won't be fishing today. It doesn't matter. Right now, let's thank God for saving you."

Boone heard his grandpa's voice crack. He looked up and saw tears in his eyes.

"Oh, Lord, thank you, thank you," his grandfather began to pray. In safety and warmth, Boone fell asleep before he heard the rest of his grandfather's deep thanks to God for rescuing him.

When the two of them arrived home to share the near-death experience of Boone, his parents had two reactions: first, great relief, and then understanding. Their next response was like Grandpa's. Boone wasn't surprised, he'd seen them act the same way with other life experiences. They knelt on the floor, held hands and thanked God for Boone and Grandpa's rescue.

When they finished, Boone's dad looked at him and said, "Son, I knew you would have some close calls in nature when I heard what you did at the campfire as a little boy."

Now Boone was puzzled. He forgot the feeling of ice-cold water and the near panic he'd felt.

"Dad," he said, "What do you mean?"

His dad nodded. All he said was, "Let me tell you about the campfire when you were two."

Chapter 1

It Began at the Campfire

"For since the creation of the world God's invisible qualities—his eternal power and divine nature—have been clearly seen, being understood from what has been made, so that men are without excuse."
— Romans 1:20

Boone was just over two years old when his family noticed. It happened outside, both the noticing and the discovery. As time passed, the family decided this was part of Boone's God-given gifts. He liked being outside. More than that, Boone was attentive to all things-nature. Every part of creation captured his attention.

Boone's grandfather would tell you he first noticed it before Boone was two. He said it was Boone's deep interest in birds. Then he would tell you the campfire story and say it was the campfire that proved to him Boone would find delight in creation in all of his days.

As Boone's grandfather grew older, the lure of a ring of stones with a wood fire in the center was an ever-increasing pleasure. Sitting still beside a fire outside that both warmed and provided an ever-changing light show were two things Boone's grandpa enjoyed.

If you asked him, Grandpa would also tell you he enjoyed the quiet that came with a fire outside. If you asked him again,

Grandpa would eventually get to the fact that people watching a fire often became thoughtful and quiet. That was important to him.

On the morning of the discovery, Boone's grandfather was alone beside a campfire. It started as a fire to burn scrap wood, but Boone's grandfather could never allow any fire to be unappreciated. That morning was the first day of fall coolness. It wasn't long before it became a "warm you and get you thinking" fire.

As Grandpa added logs to the fire, he was joined by Boone's older sister. She had her journal with her and sketched the fire. She turned to warm herself on the other side and sketched the leaves of a nearby tree. Grandpa was pleased and impressed. No one had told her to bring her journal out and sketch. Writing was one of her natural responses to life.

Then Boone toddled out. His little-boy voice warmed Grandpa's heart as he scooped him up. He asked Boone if he would like to sit and watch the fire. Boone's response was a quick head nod. As they settled on the camp chair, Boone's older sister announced she was going to sketch the tree near the house. Just like that, Boone and his grandfather were all alone. As Grandpa reflected years later, this was the first of a continuing series of adventures in creation he would have with Boone.

They watched the fire for a few moments. They listened to the birds calling in the forest in the coulee behind and below them. They felt the soft flow of air rising up the coulee on their faces. In comfortable silence they shared the camp chair. The fire warmed them. Soon the campfire had its influence on them both. Neither of them moved. Both were quiet.

Grandpa tells the next part of the story with emotion. He says he remembers Boone turning his head toward the coulee and whispering, "There's something down there."

Grandpa relates that his response was to turn his head the same direction as Boone's. He looked and listened. Then he thought, *there **is** something down there.* Without a thought about the rest of the family and with single-minded purpose, Boone's grandfather stood with Boone in his arms. After a last glance at the comfort and peace of the fire, Grandpa, with Boone on his arm, turned toward the coulee below. His first steps took the two of them down the slope and through the thick branches of the trees that grew thickly on the coulee slopes.

Grandpa said to Boone, "Should we go down there?" Boone nodded.

Grandpa will tell you with confidence it was Boone who urged them downward and deeper into the wildness of the coulee. With a sureness that comes from first-hand experience, Grandpa relates that he stopped to ask Boone if they should sit down. With equal assurance Grandpa recounts it was Boone who was dissatisfied with stopping. Every few steps, Grandpa stopped and asked if they should sit down. It was not until the two reached the bottom that Boone was satisfied. With gratitude, Grandpa noticed a stump perfect for sitting on. He took the two of them there and sat down. Because it was drier, he chose the edge of that wooden seat.

Thinking he would engage Boone with nature close by, Grandpa pulled over some branches for Boone to look at. Boone examined each twig quickly. But his greatest interest was the woods – the birds, the sounds – not twigs. In the bright

sunlight and mid-day calm, Boone was taking in everything "down there." It was an unforgettable moment for two kindred souls. If you asked Boone's grandpa, he could with confidence repeat numerous clear details about this time in the coulee. Most of them were about Boone and his response to creation in the coulee. They did hear birds. They saw a chickadee that Grandpa's chickadee call brought close. While Grandpa was always interested in anything in nature, his young grandson provided the real memories.

As they sat together, Grandpa thought of the improbability of a two year old sitting still for even a minute. He and Boone sat on the stump for nearly ten minutes. With a smile, Grandpa could recount with confidence the example Boone provided him of the influence of nature on the human heart. He sincerely believed time outside changed every human. Time outside quieted the human heart.

Grandpa thought about Boone's idea that "something was down there." He knew. God was present in the coulee. The power and divine nature of God were evident in the songs of the birds, the whisper of the wind in the leaves, and the warmth of the sun on their faces. Grandpa and Boone witnessed God's presence in the sow bug and tiny worms in the bark attached to the bottom of the stump. Boone looked with interest, but did not touch them.

Then, their quiet moments were broken by a wild call. Grandpa recognized it. It had the sound of wildness. It sounded like the hoot of a loon. When the sound came again, Grandpa was certain. It wasn't a loon — it was Boone's older brother. He was perfecting his personal imitation of a loon call. The quietness of the moment was broken. Smiling, Grandpa called back. Moments later, Boone's older brother had made his way to where Boone and his grandpa were sitting on the stump.

"Time for lunch!" Boone's brother announced.

The announcement broke the silence and their concentration. Grandpa lifted Boone to his side and stood.

"OK," was his simple response. They followed Boone's brother up the coulee slope through the trees. As they walked by the campfire, Grandpa looked down into the coulee.

"Boone," he said, "there *is* something down there."

Boone nodded and said, "We found it, Grandpa."

Chapter 2

Boone's Morning

"Let all the earth fear the LORD; let all the people of the world revere him. For he spoke, and it came to be; he commanded, and it stood firm."
— Psalm 33:8-9

As far back as he could remember in his 12-year-old life, Boone had liked being outside. This morning was no different. He was taking his first solo hike for three hours in a 10,000-acre park. Tatanka Park had been returning to nature for nearly 50 years. He was ready. He'd been outside since he was old enough to walk. His memories went back to a faded one into the coulee with his grandpa when he was little. Ever since, his father and grandfather had carefully taught him to be observant and he knew how to listen to life outside. Boone could walk quietly. He knew his way in the woods.

It was not always this way. The experience Boone was ready to enjoy came with a price tag. You see, Boone had a problem. Actually, he had more than one. One was his pride. Another was his stubbornness. Put these two together and Boone had a third problem: he would not listen. He wanted to do things *his* way. If you tried to explain Boone's problem in a few words, "It's all about me!" would sum it up.

Pride and stubbornness did not make Boone unusual. These two problems effect every human, adult or child. Boone's attitude and strong will made things difficult for his parents sometimes. And until recently, they had affected Boone seriously. Boone's "all about me" philosophy affected everyone in his family – and mostly Boone.

It had been a difficult time for Boone. Yet, he knew. He understood. When his parents brought up his pride and stubbornness, he stubbornly denied it. When he was younger, he would not listen. But his parents did not give up. They patiently endured Boone's stubborn selfishness. They did not give up instructing him.

As Boone grew older, they sat him down and talked with him. Beyond that, they also invited his grandparents to join them in keeping the truth in front of Boone: he was stubborn, and full of pride. It made him disobedient. His mom and dad often admitted to Boone the only thing they knew to do that could help Boone was to pray for him.

"We bring you to God. We tell Him what He already knows about you. Then we say, may your will be done with Boone, and may your kingdom come in his life. May Boone come to realize that life is not 'all about me.'"

Boone clearly remembered that sunny morning his parents told him their new plan. When his dad finished speaking, Boone remembered his defensive answer: "That's not fair, Dad, you know all the other kids are stubborn and want their own way. I'm not the only one."

Like it happened yesterday, Boone remembered what his dad said in reply: "We believe God has answered our prayers for you, Boone."

Suddenly Boone found himself completely focused on his dad's words.

His dad cleared his throat. Boone knew that meant he was nervous, and had something important to say. Boone became completely still.

Dad began, "We've decided to give God's answer a name. We call it 'Power Check.' Before you say anything, allow me to explain. The three of us know it has not been easy to get along with you when all you can see is doing things *your* way. You know better than we do the things we've tried to teach you – to be respectful and obey us. We think 'Power Check' is something that will motivate you and help you be willing to listen and obey more often until it becomes the way you live."

Boone could not keep his comment to himself. He interrupted, "OK, maybe you are right Dad, but would you please explain what this 'Power Check' thing is?"

His dad cleared his throat again.

Boone thought, *Wow, twice in the same conversation, dad is really nervous.* Suddenly, he decided to sit down on the family room couch. He crossed his arms. His mom and dad slowly sat in the other chairs of the room. It was quiet. Boone heard a robin out the window. He knew they were eating the fall-ripened flowering crab apples and wished he could watch them instead. His dad's voice was soft when it came.

"Boone, 'Power Check' is really simple. We've turned you and your behaviors over to God. 'Power Check' is for you. It's time you spend outside. We'll plan things regularly that will get you outside, for hours at a time. The first one is a solo hike in Tatanka Park. Your grandpa will take you, drop you off, and pick you up three hours later. But before that can happen, we want to see you working to become obedient. We want to hear "yes" rather than "no' when we ask you to do things. We want your homework done and your drums practiced every day. We want arguing with us to stop – today. Boone, we want you to pick up your clothes in your room." His dad took a deep breath.

Before his dad could say any more, Boone said, "I'll do it." He was already thinking about 'Power Check.' A solo hike? He could only imagine how fun that would be.

He heard his dad's voice saying, "Boone, 'Power Check' is when we expect you to spend time outside and search for God's invisible qualities, His *'eternal power and divine nature.'*"

The puzzled look on Boone's face prompted his dad to explain. "Boone, in the Bible book of Romans, Paul wrote these words, '*...since the creation of the world God's invisible qualities—his eternal power and divine nature—have been clearly seen, being understood from what has been made, so that people are without excuse.*'

Boone, 'Power Check' is about you spending time outside searching for evidence of God's power and love for you. We believe what these words tell us. You can understand who God is from examining His creation. When you begin to see God in Creation, He will do His work in you. As we have read the Bible and spent time in prayer, we have talked with you about what is important. That's what 'Power Check' is all about.

But first, you earn your time outside by responsible behavior. The new Boone is respectful, responsible and willing. The new Boone is an explorer who does things outside to find out who God is."

It was not an overnight success. Boone could not seem to change. His parents would ask, he would become stubborn. He almost gave up. His parents prayed. But God worked on his heart. One day Boone realized he did not feel stubborn or angry when his mom and dad asked him to do something. The next day his parents told him about this solo trip. He thought, *maybe I could change*. That was last week.

Today was solo day.

This was the first time Boone would go alone. His grandfather would drop him off. The drop-off spot was just an approach, a little driveway that ended at the woods. He had his cell phone compass to keep his bearing, but he planned to walk due north. He also had a small pocket compass in case something happened to the phone. There was a lake three-fourths of a mile distant. Boone planned to see it.

His grandpa would be back in three hours. Though his mission was a "Power Check," Boone also knew he needed to obey. It was his first test. Could he listen, could he obey? He knew he would be tempted to stay out longer. He knew his pride would tell him he could take extra time.

Boone looked into his grandpa's eyes. He saw them tear up. But he heard Grandpa's strong voice, "You know what to do, enjoy this Boone. I'll be waiting here three hours from now like we planned."

Boone just nodded. He put his hand on Grandpa's arm. His smile said thanks. Boone turned to the woods while his grandfather drove away. The wind was strong at his back, at times it gusted over 20 miles an hour. It made a roar in the tops of the trees. Boone liked it. He did not like that the wind would move his scent in front of him long before he could see the wildlife that made this magnificent hardwood forest home. In spite of that, he determined to be ultra-quiet as he moved northward toward the lake that was his morning destination.

Boone paused after his steps had taken him far enough from the road that he could not be seen. One thing he liked about the first few minutes in a wild place was the sense of the unknown. He did not know what he would see or hear. This mystery never got old. He gazed around him in a 360-degree arc, taking in the whole woods. It smelled good here. The roar of the wind was muted. His heart swelled; this was better than he expected already.

He took a deep breath and silently said, *"God strengthen me to keep my word and be back in three hours...no, before three hours. Help me, God, to be back here early."* Boone took two steps and stopped. Out loud, he said, "Did I just pray?"

He took out his phone and turned on the compass. He knew he was facing north. But he knew Grandpa would want him to check. North, it was. He carefully stored his phone in a zipped pocket. He took another deep breath of sweet forest air. Somewhere ahead lay the deep lake that was his morning destination.

He smiled and thought, *I could do solo hikes like this for the rest of my life.* Once more he slowly scanned the trees for any sign of life. He really wanted to see a whitetail deer.

Then he took his next steps.

Chapter 3

Boone's Morning Completed

*"...have you ever given orders to the morning, or shown the dawn its place,
that it might take the earth by the edges and shake the wicked out of it?"*
— Job 38:12-13

Boone scanned the woods as he carefully took each step. He had learned the art of feeling the earth before he put his full weight on it. If a twig or branch was beneath, he moved his foot to the side. There was no sound of twigs or branches breaking when Boone walked. The leaves were something else. They carpeted the floor of the woods. He could not avoid them. He could pick up his feet and place them gently on the leafy mat that was part of the woods. He did not mind that walking took longer this way. Being quiet was his goal. He intended to see things.

He had walked 100 yards when he came to the small flow of water. Crossing a stream was a delight. This one had ice on the edges and Boone's alert eyes noticed the movement of the water beneath the crystal-clear ice. Water moving under ice was a favorite sight of his. He paused. His eyes took in the liquid beauty flowing silently below him. He looked up and picked his crossing place. Deer had crossed here too. Their tracks gave him evidence – some were fresh.

As he reached the top of the little stream bank, he took a long look to the north through the woods. It was easy to see ahead. The trees in the woods were thick, but with the leaves down the late fall view was uncluttered. Nothing moved. He was reminded then of the strength of the south wind as a fresh gust bent the tops of the trees. He could hear it growl as it tore through the limbs above his head. He knew his scent went before him. He resolved to be more careful, even more quiet. He began to look for a place to sit.

He chose another landmark in one of the trees to the north. This time it was a large cluster of basswoods, the only one like it. Quietly, with care, he moved northward to the trunks bunched like only basswood grows. He noticed the near perfect rings of holes drilled by a sapsucker woodpecker in the trunk. He liked the symmetry found in the woods too. Finding it many places on different things was one of the other pleasures of being in the woods. Soundlessly, he moved to the north side of the basswood. He saw the trunks made a perfect spot to sit. One of them would make a great backrest. But the ground was bare. He decided to pick up a handful of leaves to pad his seat and keep him dry. Even with the wind noise, the rustle they made disturbed the deep stillness. He did not pick up any more – he would sit on bare earth.

Quietly he sat down, his back against one of the basswood trunks. He was on the south side of a bowl-like dip in the forest floor. He could see everything to the north. He would sit here and watch. Sitting outside always relaxed him. As the minutes passed, Boone became drowsy. But he did not let himself sleep. He'd been quiet. He'd traveled slowly, observing while he moved.

Perhaps there was a deer standing nearby. Slowly, he swiveled his head from east to west, then back again. Nothing moved. The gusting rumble of the south wind continued. He waited, eyes open and alert. He felt full of life. Adventures like this he could picture himself doing over and over. He watched and listened. Still nothing. He knew he needed to keep moving. He was not sure how much farther to the north the lake was.

Softly he rose from his leafy seat. For his next landmark, he picked another smaller clump of basswood trunks visible across the shallow bowl of forest floor ahead of him. His northward steps were silent with only a slight leaf rustle. Boone had learned much about travel in the woods. He was sure the lake was ahead. He was eager to see it.

After reaching the second basswood clump, a burl on a birch tree became his landmark to lead him further north. Reaching the birch, he glanced north once more. He could see the blue-gray color of ice on the lake. He did not need to pick another north-facing landmark now. He silently made his way to the lake.

Just before reaching the downslope towards the water, he crossed two deer trails. He had not seen any trails on the way to the lake. Yet these two paralleled the lake shore and they were only a few yards apart. But he did not dwell long on the deer trails. His eyes were pulled to the vista of the lake before him. He was amazed at the small hump of land that formed an island in the lake. It was entirely tree covered. In the mid-morning sun, it glowed.

Movement on the north end of the island shifted his gaze. A bird of prey drifted southward against the wind. He watched as the wind lifted it westward and behind the island out of sight.

He lingered on the edge of the lake for a few moments. The hike had been worth the effort. His reward was not the sighting of a deer, mink or even the fisher he knew lived in the park. His reward was something he knew he would picture again over and over in his memory. The pristine lake, its shoreline undeveloped, and the feeling of wildness were his rewards. He made plans to return for a longer hike next time.

Now it was time to meet his grandfather. He knew the way back and how long it would take him. He turned and faced into the wind. He still hoped to get a glimpse of a white-tail deer now that his scent would be covered by the onrushing wind.

Boone resolved he would come back. There was much more to learn about this place. It was a better-than-usual morning. He thought about what his parents called "Power Check." Was he witnessing the power of God? Maybe.

Harder than seeing God's power was seeing God's divine nature. How could he understand the divine nature of God? Was it the roar of the wind in the trees above? Or could it be the vast quiet he sensed in Tatanka Park? Did the silent soaring of that bird of prey show the divine nature of God? Was it found in all of them? Boone decided he couldn't find an answer. Not yet.

Then he remembered his promise to his grandfather. He would not keep Grandpa waiting. He turned south to retrace his steps. He would be as careful returning as he was on the journey to where he was. Now he knew the landmark trees. His backtrack would be easier and faster. He paused for brief seconds, but these were for careful observing glances into the woods surrounding him. He knew he was not the only living thing out here. The ever-present chickadees did not distract Boone. His mind was on seeing white-tailed deer. The trails he'd seen just before reaching the lake told him they were here. Then he thought of an even better sight – the glistening brown fur belonging to a fisher. While cautious, with eyes watchful, Boone had a promise to keep with his grandfather.

Just as he thought of his promise to Grandpa, he was gripped by a flash of anger. Why should he go back early? He knew his way in these woods, he was safe. It would not hurt his grandpa if he had to wait a few extra minutes. An extra half hour would give him a better chance to see a white-tail.

He paused, leaned against a maple tree, and thought. He wanted to sit down again. He almost did. Then he could see his grandpa's face. In that moment, all that mattered was pleasing Grandpa. He quickened his step.

Quiet and observant, Boone was nearly back to the approach when he heard the rustle of leaves to the west and south. Quickly his eyes searched toward the sound. Then he saw it. Trotting with the grace and stealth only a white-tail has, a doe moved swiftly up the low tree-covered hill and out of his view.

When Grandpa drove into the approach 15 minutes later, Boone was sitting on a log reliving what he had seen. The tawny brown image of the deer, the deep blue of the sky above the island on the lake, and the powerful sound of the wind above him all replayed in his thoughts. Before they talked, the smile on Boone's face told his grandfather that the solo hike was a success.

Grandpa's first words to Boone were those of praise, "Boone, I am certainly proud of you! Here you are waiting for me. It shows you understand what obedience looks like."

Boone answered softly, "I imagined your face, Grandpa, looking at me, and I didn't want to disappoint you."

Boone was surprised by his grandpa's answer. "Boone, you needed to see this morning created by God. Seeing is believing. Now, think about this."

Then Boone listened as Grandpa quoted some verses from the book of Job. Grandpa quoted, "*Have you ever commanded the morning to appear and caused the dawn to rise in the east? Have you made daylight spread to the ends of the earth, to bring an end to the night's wickedness?*"

For a moment Boone was silent as the words from the Bible settled on his heart. Then, in a soft voice Grandpa had to strain to hear, Boone said, "Grandpa, I saw that happen this morning."

Chapter 4

Across the Frozen Lake

"The breath of God produces ice, and the broad waters become frozen."
— Job 37:10

Love of time outside encouraged Boone to control his stubborn pride and disrespectfulness. He found the idea of a Power Check appealed more and more to him also. After his first solo hike in Tatanka State Park, Boone had told his grandpa about three of his discoveries of the power of God as they drove home that day weeks earlier. He actually found himself excited to share them with his parents when he got home. And he did.

With the sound of the wind in the tops of the trees still fresh in his memory, he described its power to his parents. Boone was surprised to see them become still, their eyes on him. Usually, he was the still person when he talked with his parents, but that was because he was being mulish with them. Now they were still, eyes on him. This was not an "about me" moment. It was about God.

He decided to share the second discovery of God's invisible power. He told them it was the silence that proved stronger than the wind as he sat at the base of the clump of basswood trees. He said he thought he could feel the silence.

His dad blinked, then nodded slowly. He watched his mom's mouth open, but no words came. Boone found himself without words as he remembered the quiet with the roar of the wind overhead. He decided that his parents would not be interested in the third thing and stopped talking.

"Boone you told us there were three things, his mother said, "You haven't shared the third thing."

Boone was surprised – they were really interested. He surprised himself too. Sharing with his parents had become important. It felt good thinking about others. Before, sitting together just talking with them made him instantly restless. Now he realized he wanted them to know how the Power Check had caused him to begin to see the "invisible qualities of God."

"Well, the third thing I could not hear or feel. I saw it." Boone noticed both of his parents had leaned forward to listen. He began. "The third thing was blue, gray, silvery, and completely covered in sunlight yellow. It was a maple-tree-covered, egg-shaped island surrounded by the deep blue of a small lake. All of this was beneath a bluebird-blue sky. As I watched, I noticed a hawk soaring to the north. Everything was still. I know I stood there just staring for a time. It was beautiful. I think beauty shows God's power too. What do you think?"

Boone was shocked. Now he was asking for his parent's opinions!

His dad just smiled, nodded his head and said, "You also saw God's divine nature. God is awesome, He makes beautiful things because He loves us."

That was ten days ago.

Boone had been thinking his parents had forgotten about time outside and Power Check. He was surprised to see his dad at the kitchen counter as he walked through the back door. He relished Friday afternoons after school. He enjoyed the fact that he could stay up longer before bed, and sleep later the next morning.

Seeing his father sitting at the counter was a delight for Boone. Usually, his dad came home from work just before the family's evening meal.

He saw a package of graham crackers and two glasses of milk on the counter in front of his dad. His dad liked graham crackers and milk as well as Boone did. They were often his first choice for after school treats. Sometimes he snapped them in sections and dunked them, sometimes he crushed them in the glass, poured milk over them and ate them with a spoon. Dunking graham crackers required good judgement and timing: too soon and they were not soft, too late and the milk-soaked section dropped into the glass. Then he had to get a spoon to fish out the sunken piece. Boone thought of it as a graham cracker contest. Sometimes the cracker won...it was not fun to lose to a cracker.

"Hi, Dad," Boone said with enthusiasm he meant, "did you take off work early today?"

Boone's father patted his son's shoulder and smiled. "Yes, I did. I needed to tell you something important, it can't wait till evening. Your mom and I feel you've earned your next Power Check. Tomorrow morning, we think you should cross Ironwood Lake by yourself."

Boone could only smile, his mind was already on the ice. This was a great idea. Boone was in bed earlier, even though it was Friday night. He planned to get up early the next morning.

Boone liked mornings. He liked adventure. This morning had come quickly. He'd been thinking about this adventure since eating graham crackers with Dad yesterday. He would cross the lake. He would do it walking on ice. He knew experts called ice a film on water. But he had been watching the lake. Ice had covered its surface three weeks earlier. It had never opened since.

He would be careful. He told his dad. He told his mom. He knew what they would say, and both did: "Be careful, I love you."

Across the frozen lake was where he anticipated adventure. But when he crossed the lake, he knew there would be adventure on the ice as well. He'd walked on ice-covered water before. He knew ice could be unsafe, so he would be safe and walk around the very edge. The water was not over his head there. He knew his first exploration would be on the ice. That would make two explorations in one. That was even better. These quests would happen this morning.

It was a cold morning. One of Boone's daily habits was to check the family's digital thermometer each morning when he got out of bed. His first glance at the device showed 14° F. He would leave after breakfast.

In his young life, he had been faithfully taught by both parents and grandparents that the Bible is God's Word. Before breakfast and before final preparation to start these adventures, he picked up his Bible. This morning he read these words from Psalm 33, "*Let all the earth fear the Lord; let all the people of the world revere him. For he spoke, and it came to be...*"

Boone could not fully understand how God could just speak and things came to be. This morning he thought he would walk among the things God spoke into being.

He became more and more eager to be on his way. He took time to eat a first-rate breakfast. He even ate a banana. That's when his mom reminded him explorers brush their teeth before great expeditions. Sometimes he debated his mother about brushing. Not this morning, he was keen on getting started. He brushed, without discussion.

Before his dad left the house, he reminded Boone about dressing in layers. It was on his mind as he put his toothbrush away. When he walked through the kitchen his mom said, "The thermometer reads 15 degrees Boone, remember to layer up." He knew if his grandpa were there, he would hear the same thing.

His first layer was a one-piece suit of long underwear. It was old, but it was lightweight and warm. He added a thermal turtle neck and pulled on two pair of socks; one pair was made of wool. Over his cargo pants he added an outer layer of waterproof wind pants. For his arms and chest, he added a fleece vest and a lightweight parka with a hood. Once his insulated, waterproof boots were slipped on, he would step outside. He did not plan to bring the survival bag his grandfather helped him assemble after his first solo trip. He was close to home. He would rely on his cell phone. He'd checked the charge on the battery.

As he stepped out the door, he reached the willow walking stick his grandfather had made for him last Christmas. Boone felt his grandfather was near when the stick was in hand. Grandpa's signature, burned in the wood near the top, confirmed it.

After he had said goodbye to his mother, he'd stepped into the crisp early winter air before he remembered. How many times had he heard his dad and grandfather say never head onto early ice without your ice picks. He'd left the two palm-size cylinders of wood with nails firmly fastened to the end in the drawer in the laundry. The nylon cord attached to the other end of each cylinder went around his neck. If he accidentally broke through the ice, he could use the ice picks to pull himself back to safety. He knew his dad would ask. His trip across the frozen lake would have to wait five minutes. Since he did not see his mom anywhere, he kept his boots on to walk into the laundry. Boone thought to himself, *they are clean yet.*

Finally, he was ready and standing outside. Though he was now 12, Boone had already developed the habits of someone used to being outside. He stopped and gazed around him.

Boone was pleased his family lived two quick blocks from the lake. He would be there in five minutes. He decided to take big steps. He thought about those first steps on the ice. He had completely forgotten the math homework due Monday. His drums and practicing them would have to wait. It was adventure first, and the first part of the adventure would be across the frozen lake.

His steps led him westward at first. West in the direction of the sunset. As he walked, he came to the cross street that led south and east. This street edged Ironwood Lake. His mind was filled with what he would do. He reminded himself to go slow. He needed to control his emotions to make good decisions. Calm thinking produced wise choices. He knew first ice was no place for foolish thinking.

He was not only thinking about safety. He was thinking about what he would see. He remembered first ice walks on Ironwood with his father when he was younger. Boone smiled as he remembered the colors. He grinned at the thought of seeing thousands of air bubbles trapped in the ice.

His grin remained as these thoughts took him back to first ice last year. He thought of the cracks and the impressive, connected network they made. He especially enjoyed the way cracks showed the depth of the ice. By looking down on them it was possible to see from the surface of the ice to where it met the water. Not only were they beautiful, they indicated how thick it was and if the ice was safe. He'd learned about the cracks from his dad. Thinking about cracks reminded Boone that his father was a good teacher.

The last house along the lake was his point of entry to its ice. His dad knew the people who lived there. They enjoyed Boone's enthusiasm for nature and even gave permission for him to walk on the edge of their lawn down to the lake. Boone was grateful. He reached the edge of the lake. Its ice was in front of him. He stopped – there was a problem. The ice next to shore was dark. Just beyond it the ice was snow covered. He knew from listening to both his dad and grandfather that the dark color meant liquid water had come up on the ice. The ice at the edge could be weaker. He picked a spot where the dark color was narrow. He could step out onto the snow-covered ice. He took a big step.

The ice held; it did not even make a crack. This was Boone's first time alone on the ice. He turned and looked across the lake. The trees on the far shore looked dark. There were no houses on the other side. No one lived there. He wanted to walk in those woods. He knew this forest was home to many birds. Deer lived there. There were rumors that even the tracks of a mountain lion had been seen there. A little shiver went down Boone's spine as he stared across at the forest on the other side. He did not plan only to look. He planned to walk among the trees on that dark shore. He wanted to see and hear the birds there. He would do his own search for mountain lion tracks.

He took a deep breath of the cold brisk air of early winter and turned to walk the ice near the shore. It would be safer at the edge, even though it would take longer to get to the wood. His dad had been very clear that Boone should stay at the shore edge. Boone thought again to himself, *it's easier and here on ice, safer to obey the first time.*

The stumps of trees frozen in the ice took his mind off the adventure awaiting him in the trees. As he walked closer, he could see the tracks of an animal that had gone there before him. Because they were filled with snow, he knew the animal had been here a few days earlier. He also knew that because they were a single line of tracks that a coyote likely made them. The thought of walking where a coyote had gone before added mystery. Boone wondered what the coyote had been hunting.

The last tree stump was very weathered, its bark gone. A short branch pointed out into the lake. Boone wondered how many birds had perched on this shelf of wood just above the water. He forgot about the coyote. His eyes drifted over the surface of the stump – wind and water had smoothed its surface.

As he walked past the stump, he saw the cattails on the shore's edge ahead of him. They gracefully swayed in the northwest wind. Their movement and color drew him. The golden cattail stalks were a beautiful contrast to the white snow he walked on. He wondered what animals moved in and out on the ice beneath these towering aquatic plants lining this part of the lake shore. He thought a mink would find this area interesting. Mink eat muskrats, and muskrats would come here to eat the cattails.

While he was a bit disappointed that snow had covered the ice before he arrived, he was thankful that the white covering made walking much easier, and he reminded himself, safer. A new thought came to mind. He stopped. He realized he was missing the cracks and the air bubbles. He knelt on the snow. With his mittens, he brushed off the thin layer of snow covering the ice. It was worth the effort.

His window was too small to see many cracks. But the bubbles were there. The dark color below told him liquid water was beneath the ice. Boone wondered how so many bubbles could become trapped in the ice. He found joy in seeing bubbles in different layers of the ice. The faint blue color and the random placement of bubbles was beauty he enjoyed. While he marveled at the miracle and beauty of ice, he remembered that he had not heard one crack as he walked. He relaxed a bit. The ice would hold and he would stay safe – and dry.

But he would still walk near the shore. He would not take any unwise chances. He lifted his head toward the trees standing silently on the far shore. Yes, the ice would hold him. Soon, he would walk in those dark trees. He did not know what he would see next, but he knew it would be wonderful. It was time to be moving.

Chapter 5

Into the Forest

*"They will celebrate your abundant goodness
and joyfully sing of your righteousnesss."*
— Psalm 145:7

As Boone made the final steps toward the forested shore, the sky began to lighten. He felt the wind on his cheeks. That meant a wind shift – to the south – this would be very good for him. His scent would be carried away to the north.

He thought, *If I am quiet and move slowly, I just may see more than birds.* As he reached the shore, the first late morning rays of sunlight brightened his path. A smile came to his lips. With the sun out, he would be able to see better in the woods. Glancing down to where the shore met the ice edge, he saw dark ice on this side too.

To himself he repeated, *dark ice means thin ice.* Avoiding the dark ice, he chose the rock imbedded in the shore as his next step to land.

Onshore, he stopped and took a deep breath. He was both relieved and excited. He now knew the trip home back across the ice would be safe. The thought occupying his mind now was, *What is ahead of me, what will I see?*

His grandfather's words came next, "God puts a surprise outside for you every day. Will you be out there to see it?"

He was.

He took another deep breath and let it out slowly. He reminded himself to be calm. He determined to walk slowly and stop often. Carefully he stepped into the trees. He glanced behind. The sunlight now illuminated the trees on the south side of every trunk. Light and shadow were everywhere. The snow-covered lake ice in the background made his heart surge. Boone was amazed. Why did sights like this thrill his heart?

He took another deep breath. This one came from awe. He wondered, *Would this be the daily surprise Grandpa always told him to seek? Was this beauty part of God's divine nature or infinite power?*

Then he remembered something he should have done before stepping into the forest. He looked around, then around the trees near the tops. He'd forgotten to check for the mountain lion. He scanned slowly and carefully in a complete circle. He made no sound. As he came back to his starting place, he let out a slow breath. It was relief. No mountain lion in view.

He was ready to move farther south. He decided to stay at the edge of the trees. He was thankful he did, but this came later. Coming to a clear-cut swath in the forest, he stopped and looked behind him again. Washed in the winter sunlight was an iron-wood tree. It still had rich-brown leaves clinging to some of its branches. He stood and admired the shape and silhouette of the tree. He noticed how it grew more to the east and less on the west side of the tree. Of course, there was more sunlight toward the clear-cut. Was this his surprise?

He thought of Grandpa's other advice, "You'll know which was your surprise when you get home and think about what you saw."

He turned to face west. He decided to walk west along the clear-cut. He had only taken two steps when his eyes picked up a brown mass about 100 yards ahead. Boone had learned to estimate distances outside from his dad. Now, he was thankful he had listened. He stood, focused on what was ahead of him. Having spent considerable time outside with Dad and Grandpa, Boone knew this brown mass did not fit in with the forest surroundings. It was neither tree nor brush. It moved.

Boone's senses went into hyper-alert. Slowly, he lowered himself to his knees. Another of his dad's lessons flashed through his mind: *Keep low.*

As he watched, unsure of what this animal was, he saw a second brown mass. A moment later, it moved too. Then he saw an ear flick. Just as quickly, he could make out the head of the animal. It was a deer. By its size, Boone guessed it was possibly a yearling. It looked small. He watched the second brown mass. It was a deer. Boone's next thought: *These are twins.*

Boone did not notice his breathing. He forgot the south wind on his left cheek. He forgot the ironwood tree and the light and shadows with the lake behind. He never thought to check for the mountain lion. He knew he did not need to wait until he was home to know what his surprise was. It was the deer.

He froze.

A moment later one of the deer lifted its head and pointed its ears toward him. Boone understood this one knew he was there. He remembered his earlier decision to stay along the edge

of the trees. He was thankful for that and for the wind blowing his scent away from the ultra-sensitive noses of the deer.

As he watched, Boone believed that God directed his steps. He had been taught this since he was old enough to understand. He smiled now at the realization that he had experienced God leading him now. He marveled at the scene before him.

While one deer watched, the other picked at something on the ground. When they slowly began to move toward him, Boone anticipated them coming much closer. His heart beat faster. While they slowly edged closer, the same deer kept its eyes and its ears on the alert.

He was disappointed when just as smoothly they began to move into the forest to his right. It was not long before both had blended perfectly with their surroundings. Tree trunks, branches and brown grass in light and shadow enabled the brown deer twins to disappear.

After they were gone, Boone was still kneeling. He was savoring, totally enjoying the wonderful sight he had just witnessed. Moments passed with Boone deep in thought.

Later he came to a decision. It was time to go home. While he had not explored this wild place fully, he knew he had witnessed and delighted in his "God-made nature surprise." He would go home. On the way he would relive the seconds with the white-tails. His walk across the ice seemed routine now. He couldn't wait to share his afternoon story with his family. He'd seen more than birds!

As he stepped on the ice, he remembered some of his responsibilities. He had a drum. He had a math book in his backpack. He would practice the drum and do his homework without being reminded, he would. Boone smiled. Right now, two things made him happy. It felt good being responsible, and he knew that also meant his next power check would come sooner!

Chapter 6

Spearfishing
with Pastor Andrew

"A friend loves at all times, and a brother is born for adversity."
— Proverbs 17:17

It came after Christmas. Boone was beginning to wonder if the busy Christmas season had caused his parents to forget about scheduling another power check. They hadn't forgotten the last time. But this time seemed longer. It had been a month already. He'd been patient and kind, and he'd been careful with his tongue. He had shown his parents respect. As far as his being responsible, his mom had only reminded him once to pick up his clothes. Boone thought they had forgotten about power checks for sure.

He knew something was up the next afternoon when he saw his dad at the kitchen table with two glasses of milk and a package of graham crackers.

His dad wanted to talk. Graham crackers and milk was the favorite snack for both of them. While dunking his grahams in milk, Boone heard his dad say the words he'd been waiting for. "Boone, your mother and I think it is time for your next power check. We have an idea that will get you outside. We think you should go ice fishing."

As long as he could remember, Boone had enjoyed fishing. He couldn't remember the first time his dad had taken him, but he was a little boy then. Boone's grandpa was partly responsible for his grandson's pleasure in fishing. He and Boone spent hours on the water in summertime.

Boone already had a sizable knowledge of how to catch fish. He knew about the best time of day to fish, habitat and fish responses to weather. He was beginning to understand how water temperature and oxygen levels effected fish. While he did not realize it, he had knowledge equal to many fishing experts.

He also had begun to acquire something else: humility. With patience and prayer, his father and grandfather taught him to love God with all his heart, mind and strength. Both men were delighted as they observed Boone gradually accept the truth about God which they taught him. They knew it did not always work that way in human hearts.

It helped to have Boone outside with them. They marveled with him at sunrises and sunsets. All three found awe in every part of creation. The two most important men in Boone's life knew part of the reason Boone accepted their showing him about humility was because the boy knew God as Creator of all things.

This winter there would come a third man to teach him.

Earlier that winter, Pastor Andrew brought a rich new feature to Boone's life. One morning after church, Grandpa introduced Boone to Pastor Andrew. Grandpa said Boone would like what Pastor Andrew had to say. Boone knew Grandpa did not like fishing in cold weather. He did not like walking on a frozen lake.

"It's slippery, its full of cracks, and I might fall in," he said. Boone had asked his grandpa to take him ice fishing many times. Grandpa always said, "No."

Boone's dad didn't like to ice fish either. When Boone would ask, his dad would say, "Too cold!"

Pastor Andrew liked the cold. Even better, he liked ice fishing.

"Boone, I have someone I'd like you to meet," his grandpa said. Boone looked into the twinkling blue eyes of another grandpa. He was a striking man with a well-trimmed mustache. The man held out his hand to Boone. When Boone took his hand, he felt power. He already knew one thing, this man was strong.

"Boone, this is Pastor Andrew. He and his wife have moved here from Canada," his grandpa said with a smile. The voice Boone heard next was deep, clear and strong.

"Hello, Mr. Boone," said Pastor Andrew with a grin on his face. "I understand you would like to go ice fishing, but these two men here think it's either not safe or too cold. Would you go with me?"

Boone couldn't believe it. Two thoughts came to him at once. A chance to go ice fishing! But he didn't know this man. He did'nt know what to do.

He turned to his dad. "Would it be OK if I went ice fishing with Pastor Andrew, Dad?" he asked.

His dad's answer filled him with gladness.

"Sure, son, Pastor Andrew will be a great ice fishing partner for you."

With pleasure in his eyes, Boone returned his gaze to Pastor Andrew. "Yes sir, I would be happy fish with you. Actually, when can we go?"

Pastor Andrew looked down at Boone from his six-foot height and said, "You can call me Andrew. Would you like to try to spear a fish tomorrow?"

Boone heard Pastor Andrew when he said, "Call me Andrew," but for some reason – perhaps it was out of respect – Boone never could call him Andrew.

Boone couldn't believe how good this was. He'd just met Pastor Andrew, or, Andrew! Boone knew what to do, "Dad, could I help him try spear a fish tomorrow? I don't have school this week."

His dad just smiled. Then he said, "Yes, you can. You've been wanting to do this for a long time. Oh, Boone, there is one thing you need to do before you go with Pastor Andrew. Tomorrow morning, please take out the garbage before the garbage truck comes."

Wow!, Boone thought, *my room is messy too, but I can take out the garbage.*

"I'll do it tonight, Dad," Boone said with a great smile covering his face. He decided then to pick up the clothes on the floor his mom had been telling him about for the last week. If he had anything to do about it, nothing would prevent this fishing trip with Pastor Andrew, uh...Andrew. He was finding it hard to use this dignified man's first name only.

"Well, young man, Boone is it?" said Pastor Andrew, "I will come by your home tomorrow at 8:30 a.m. Be ready, and wear your cold weather gear."

Boone felt a hand on his shoulder. Turning, he faced his dad.

"Time to go home son," he softly said.

Boone was already distracted. Tomorrow would not come soon enough. He forgot he was hungry. He was already thinking he would not be able to sleep. He could see fish swimming in the cold lake water.

As they walked, Boone remembered that before fishing, he had responsibilities. There were clothes he was absolutely picking up, and a garbage can he would wheel to the curb. He could think about fish in cold, clear water while he did his chores. As he thought about those clothes on his floor, he decided that hanging them up right away would give him more time to do what he enjoyed most...think about fishing. There was only one thing better than thinking about it, and that was actually fishing.

Boone realized Pastor Andrew may be a new friend. Friendship was a gift Boone considered a prize.

Chapter 7

A Spear in His Hand

"He is like a man building a house, who dug down deep and laid the foundation on rock. When a flood came, the torrent struck that house but could not shake it, because it was well built."
— Luke 6:48

Boone's eyes popped open. What time was it? Had he overslept? What if Pastor Andrew had already come, and had gone on without him?

Immediately he turned his head to the clock at his bedside. With a sigh he lay his head on his pillow again. It was Monday, 6:00 a.m. Then Boone remembered with a smile – no school today!

Since Pastor Andrew would not be coming until 8:30 a.m., Boone had two and a half hours to get ready. But except for breakfast and getting dressed, he was ready. He was ready when he went to bed last night. His boots, warm stocking cap, heavy coat, thermal pants and wool socks were by the door. Stuffed in one sleeve of his coat, his leather chopper mitts with wool liners were ready for him to take out. The garbage can was already at the curb and not one shirt or pair of pants were on his floor, not even a sock.

He knew he could sleep till 7:00 and have time to be ready. But he could not. Quietly he got out of bed and in the before sunrise darkness of his room he put on his base layer of clothing. Just as quietly, he walked past his mom and dad's room. He knew they would be up soon, but he didn't want to wake them now. He knew what he would do before breakfast. It was something he'd seen his parents do when they first got up in the morning. He would read his Bible. He decided that after 12 years of life, he should read for himself what God said in the Bible.

It was hard to concentrate. He could still see fish swimming in cold water. He remembered reading Jesus' words about the *"wise man who built his house upon the rock"* (Luke 6:48).

Boone knew what Jesus meant when He said the *"rock."* He meant the one and only Jesus, God's Son. Boone knew that building his life on following the words of Jesus was a sure foundation. Quietly he asked for God to help him.

A second later, he was thinking about a hole in the ice and those fish he knew would be swimming in the cold water below. He checked the clock, it was only 6:30! He breathed a deep sigh... time was going so slowly.

He jumped when he felt a hand on his shoulder and heard his mother say, "Would you like an omelet for breakfast?"

By 8:00 that morning, Boone had finished breakfast, brushed his teeth (after his mother reminded him there was time), and had all his warm gear on. He stood at the door waiting for Pastor Andrew.

Wisely, his dad said, "Boone, since you have all your warm clothes on you can wait outside. That way you will see Pastor Andrew when he comes."

With a quick hug and, "Goodbye, I love you," Boone was out the door.

He ducked out of his mother's hug before she could kiss him. Outside, he checked the bird feeders in the back yard. He filled the two that were low on seed, keeping a part of his attention on the front driveway of the house.

He checked his phone, the time was 8:20. Still 10 minutes before Pastor Andrew came. Waiting was so hard. Then he saw movement at the edge of his vision. It was Pastor Andrew's pickup! Boone ran to the driveway. He was surprised to see his grandpa sitting on the passenger side.

As Boone jumped into the seat in back, he said, "Grandpa, I thought you didn't like ice fishing?"

Grandpa's response made Boone glad. "I wanted to see you spear your first northern today. I even brought my camera."

Boone buckled up, he was more than excited, this was already better than he had expected.

The drive to the lake went quickly with Grandpa and Pastor Andrew talking about how deep the ice could be, how much snow there was on the ice, and the fish Pastor Andrew had been seeing. Boone thought he had never heard such fascinating things before in his life. Before he realized it, they were parking by the lake. Pastor Andrew said they would walk on the ice because it was safer than driving. Within five minutes they were on the ice.

"We can walk on water," Pastor Andrew joked.

He gave Boone the spear. The men carried the ice saw, chisel, spearing decoys and an empty five-gallon bucket. Boone knew what the bucket was for. He looked at the spear and wondered how many fish would be inside that bucket when they went home. He enjoyed wondering if they would spear a fish too big to fit in the bucket.

It took Grandpa and Pastor Andrew 40 long minutes to cut a spearing hole in the ice. Boone helped by cleaning the ice chips and chunks out of the hole.

Grandpa warned, "Careful, Boone, don't slip and fall in. That water is ice cold!"

Boone stared into the dark water. He would be careful. When the ice chips were cleaned out, the men slid the spear-house over the hole and adjusted it to fit. Grandpa shoveled snow against the ice house to keep out the light and cold air. Pastor Andrew started the little heater in the corner.

He said, "Boone, you can take off your coat and cap, hang them on the wall hook. Then you can stand behind your grandpa when he comes in."

The three of them squeezed into the spear-house – though it was small, there was room for all of them. Pastor Andrew gave Grandpa the spear. "You start," he said.

This was another surprise – Grandpa was spearing!

Boone was glad he had not said what he was thinking. He was about to say, "Shouldn't I start first? I'm supposed to spear my first fish today."

Just as quickly he realized how disrespectful that would sound. "Thank you, God, for reminding me it's not all about me," he prayed silently.

After a minute or two Boone's eyes had adjusted to the darkness in the spear-house. He leaned over Grandpa's shoulder and peered into the water. It was like looking into an aquarium. But this was a lake! Boone began to see fish...four sunfish, a bass and a black crappie swam in the clear water below them. As he looked to the edges of the hole, he realized there were other fish swimming just at the edge of his vision. Boone guessed there were at least 15 fish in sight. He was speechless.

Just then another movement caught his eye. Pastor Andrew pulled on a string that dangled into the center of the hole. At the end of the string was a small fish. But it was not alive. When Pastor Andrew lifted the string, the little fish swam in a circle. It looked like a real fish.

"It's called a decoy, Boone," said Pastor Andrew.

"I was just going to ask you what that little fish is," said Boone.

"Watch it, but keep your eye on the edges of the hole now," said Pastor Andrew, "something should happen soon."

Boone stared at the little fish decoy as Pastor Andrew had said. Then he noticed something moving in the corner of the hole in front of his grandpa's left boot. He saw the nose of a big fish, just the nose. "Look, Grandpa! It's a northern!" Boone whispered.

Even a week later Boone could remember what happened next. Slowly and quietly, Grandpa picked up the spear. He moved it over the back of the fish, just behind its head. He slowly lowered the spear into the water, then in a blink, he sent the spear dropping toward the fish. Boone knew the fish was on the spear as it wriggled to escape. He watched amazed as Grandpa pulled it up. When he lifted it out of the hole into the house, chaos broke out. The fish was big. It splashed and thrashed until Grandpa opened the door and carried it outside.

When Grandpa was outside, Pastor Andrew said, "Boone, you go out there, look at the beautiful fish your Grandpa speared."

Careful to not step in the hole, Boone stepped out into the early morning sunshine. The big northern was stunning. Its camouflaged skin had lines of gold running from head to tail. Grandpa mercifully ended its life and handed it to Boone.

"Keep your fingers out of its mouth," he warned.

Boone took the big fish in his hands. It was heavy.

Grandpa said, "This one may weigh six pounds. Put it in the pail, then use the towel to wipe the northern slime from your hands."

Boone knew the "slime" was like the northern's skin. It smelled fishy too. Grandpa went inside the little house. Boone admired the beautiful fish a moment longer before he lowered it into the pail. He realized he was alone outside.

When he opened the door, Grandpa held the spear to Boone. He said, "Now, Boone, it's your turn."

He looked at the spear in his hand. This was what he had been waiting for! Would he actually spear a fish?

Chapter 8

He Throws a Spear

*"He got up, rebuked the wind and said to the waves,
'Quiet! Be still!'
Then the wind died down and it was completely calm."*
— Mark 4:39

He looked at the spear. He nervously swallowed. Then he lowered himself onto the spearing stool. He looked at Grandpa, still holding the spear. Boone reached out his hand for the spear. It was heavier than he remembered, and he had carried it to the spear house. In his bare hand he felt the cold of the long steel handle.

He took a deep breath and he heard Pastor Andrew say, "Set the spear tines on the edge of the hole."

The handle rested on his shoulder. His eyes began to sweep the edges of the hole for a first view of a northern. Pastor Andrew reached for the string holding the decoy.

He said, "Ready, Mr. Boone?" Boone could only nod. He was already focused on the activity below him in the water. He counted six sunfish around the edges. With a slight lean to the right, he could see a bass and three more sunfish at the far-left edge of the hole. He would be alert for a change in this picture.

Pastor Andrew pulled the decoy string. It went swimming in a circle beneath them, once, twice, three times, and then Pastor

Andrew released the string. The decoy swam more slowly and soon it stopped, suspended in the center of the hole.

Boone knew that the movement of the decoy would be quickly picked up by any northern close by. He began to scan the edges. He watched for a change in the picture below him. The sunfish swam in closer to the decoy, first the six, then the three. The bass swam under the decoy and away from the hole on his right. He scanned back to the left and saw the nose of a fish. But as he watched he realized it was another sunfish. He took a silent breath, a false alarm.

Pastor Andrew broke the silence. "One could not find a better way to spend a winter afternoon than this," he said.

Though it was too dark to see, Boone could feel the smile on Pastor Andrew's face. Softly Boone replied, "I agree."

As he spoke the word "agree," Boone saw something in the right corner of the hole on Pastor Andrew's side. His boot was pointed toward the large dark green nose of a northern pike. Boone held his breath. Slowly and silently, he lifted the spear and held it above the water. The fish would need to swim into the hole further, in order for Boone to have a chance to spear it. Pastor Andrew rolled the decoy string between his thumb and forefinger. The decoy's head moved slightly away from the northern.

As Boone watched, the fish swam nearly up to the decoy. Now it was in full view, except the whole fish did not fit in the hole. Boone heard Grandpa whisper, "Big."

In the same instant, he heard Pastor Andrew whisper, "Uh-huh, it is. You can throw the spear now Boone," he added.

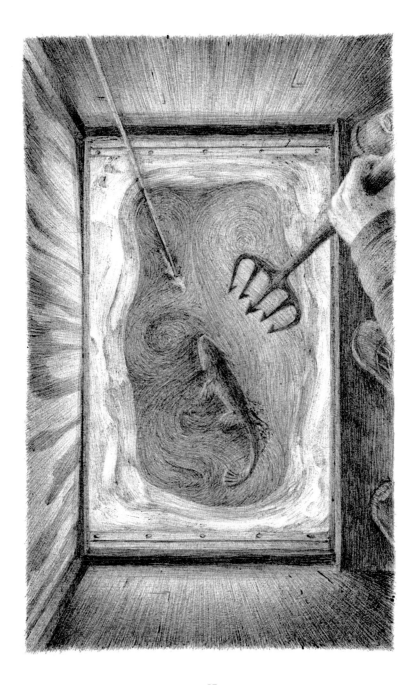

Silently Boone moved the spear to just behind the head of the big fish. Then he slowly lowered the spear into the water. Boone knew if the spear splashed into the water the fish would swim away. He had remembered what Pastor Andrew had said earlier.

With the spear just behind the head of the fish and partly into the water, Boone gave the spear a stab and released. Its weight quickly carried it toward the fish. Then the water below them began to churn. Boone saw a white flash – *fish belly*, he thought. Then he pulled on the string attached to the spear. The weight of the fish nearly pulled the string from his hand. With his other hand he reached for the end of the spear as it came up. Holding the spear was like holding a bucking horse. He put the other hand on the spear too and pulled the fish up. Boone thought the hardest part was over. He was wrong.

As the big fish was lifted up out of the water it began to flop its head and tail back and forth. Water splashed on all of them. The body of the fish slammed into the sides of the spear house.

Suddenly, things were crazy in that tiny house. All Boone could do was hold on. He was not going to let this one go. Then he felt another hand on the spear. Grandpa had reached in to help. Together they lifted the thrashing big fish toward the door. Pastor Andrew was already reaching around to get it open.

When they laid the fish on the ice, it gave a mighty heave and wrenched the spear out of their hands. The spear banged against the door of the house. Boone was off his stool in a second. On his way out of the door he barely managed to grab the spear handle and push the tines into the ice. The big fish was pinned.

Suddenly Pastor Andrew was by his side. He said, "Boone, I got it now."

Moments later the big fish had been subdued and measured. As Boone lifted the heavy fish to the pail, Pastor Andrew's joyful voice announced, "it's a seven-pounder!"

Boone felt hands slapping on his back. As he looked into their faces, he saw the two older men grinning at him. Grandpa came close and put an arm around his shoulder. "I'm proud of you, Boone! Now before you put your fish in the pail, we have a few photos to take."

Bone could feel the smile creep across his face. He knew he liked fishing, but spearing was even better – it was marvelous! He looked over to Pastor Andrew.

"Pastor Andrew, this was fantastic!" he whispered.

After the first release of the fish spear, Boone was completely captivated with spearfishing. Pastor Andrew and his grandfather knew it. Older men have wisdom to understand such things. The three of them met twice more in the little house on the ice with the giant hole into the lake. Boone called it a "triple power check."

It was late that winter that Boone began to write his experiences in a journal. After the third spearfishing trip with Pastor Andrew, Boone found a composition book on his bed. At first, he was unhappy. *More work*, he thought, *they want me to do more work!*

Then he saw the note. He read it.

"Boone, you have been responsible. Your mother and I have been very happy with how respectful you've been lately. We think power checks are helping you become a young man God delights in. We have a suggestion – write about your adventures with Pastor Andrew. Put into words the ways you see God's power and divine nature. When you write your thoughts and feelings, they become more powerful examples that give glory to God. You can use them to strengthen others on their journey with God."

Boone's mind and heart were full of the beauty he witnessed on that last spearfishing trip. The grace-filled images of fish swimming in crystal clear water were fresh. Without thinking, he picked up the journal and sat at his desk. There he found a pen and wrote his name and the date. He'd learned that from his teachers in school. What came after was all from Boone's heart. As he sat at his desk that quiet, partly-sunny Saturday afternoon, his first words were, "Thank you, God."

With each power check trip that winter, Boone found himself feeling calmer. He actually wanted to listen, and he felt closer to his parents.

What might have been the best result from each power check trip was his deepening understanding of God. Boone saw God's power in late afternoon sunsets. He heard the power of God in the wind as it swept snow against the walls of the spear house and formed pillow drifts alongside. Looking into the spear hole always thrilled him – it was another world.

Yet, the confirmation of God's presence outside came the most clearly from something Boone never expected. It was the silence of winter.

In the three times Boone spent with his grandfather and Pastor Andrew spearfishing, there was always time outside. When they walked to the spear house it was quiet. Sometimes in the spear house both Grandpa and Pastor Andrew were silent. At first, Boone was uncomfortable in the silence. He soon came to delight in it. In the silence on the wintery surface of the lake Boone felt the presence and power of God. Boone wrote about silence in his journal. Putting his thoughts on paper did not seem like work any longer. As he wrote, he longed for the next power check, and more silence.

Silence. Boone thought about silence again. What was the silence like in the boat with the disciples when Jesus calmed the storm? Boone realized it was like sitting in the spear house with Grandpa and Pastor Andrew.

Sitting at his desk, Boone remembered those winter spearing trips. He thought, *God's power is seen in the silence of winter.*

Chapter 9

The Perfect Surprise

*"Honor your father and your mother, so that you may live long
in the land the LORD your God is giving you."*
— Exodus 20:12

As Boone ended the school year that spring, he had little time
for fishing. He used it as an excuse for his behavior. The old
stubbornness, messy room and disrespect for his parents came
back. His parents were disappointed and discouraged. Boone
was too.

In the sunshine after school one day, Boone realized
something. He had been busy with school all spring. His parents
were busy with work and his older brother and sister with their
busy school lives. Boone felt forgotten. But he knew something
more important had been happening. The busy spring activities
of his family had left no time for power checks.

He was not thinking selfishly, he told himself. Power checks
enabled him to be more cooperative, and certainly more cheerful.
He tried to stop those "all about me" thoughts, but recently they
were often on his mind.

One evening, close to the end of the school year and at the
family meal, Boone brought the subject up. "Mom and Dad, I
need a power check, he calmly said.

Boone was amazed at the look of surprise he saw on his mother and father's faces.

His mom spoke first, "Boone, you are absolutely right! We have forgotten to plan power checks for you. I am sorry."

His dad apologized too. "Boone, it's my fault. I've forgotten what time outside means to you."

Boone had a thought he decided would help the current discussion, so he added it. "Maybe if I had a few power checks it would be easier for me to obey and listen? Mom and dad, I need to go fishing soon," he added.

They nodded in silence. He knew they were listening.

Just a few days later, school was out. That meant time for fishing. It meant more time outside. It meant less time in a room where he felt cramped. His teacher wasn't the problem. Boone just had difficulty being inside all day.

He breathed a relief-filled sigh as he walked home, and a second bigger sigh followed.

In his backpack were the few things he kept in his locker – a few worn-down-on-both-ends pencils, two almost-used-up spiral notebooks and a three-ring binder filled with worksheets and papers from the classes Boone had just finished.

He sighed again. Knowing school was out for the next three months felt good. No, he decided, it felt *really* good. He sighed again just because it felt so good.

His eyes scanned the sky overhead for birds. He never tired of watching any bird soar. This spring he had found delight watching the early spring spirals of hawks and sandhill cranes, and in the last few days he had discovered the American pelican was migrating. They were exceptional at soaring. When he saw nothing in the bright blue sky above him, he turned his attention to the bird song around him.

As he turned the corner to walk down the street in front of his house, he heard the "crazy robin" song of the rose-breasted grosbeak. Although it was now early June and the grosbeaks had returned in early May, Boone was thrilled to see them – or hear them – any time. He leaned against the tree where the call originated and gazed into the fresh, early season maple leaves.

He was still looking for the bird when he heard his name called. It was his mother. He felt embarrassed. Everyone in the neighborhood would think he was still a little boy. With a May birthday, he was now 13. Forgetting the rose-breasted grosbeak above him he hurried home, afraid his mother could call him again.

A few moments later he found himself apologizing to his mom for his thoughts. He found there was a very good reason she was calling him so the whole neighborhood could hear. She had good news for him. She had seen him stopped by the maple tree and couldn't wait to share the good news. She called because she knew Boone would be excited.

His grandpa and grandma had called, she said. They knew today was Boone's last day of school before the summer break. His mom said they had a request of Boone. She said they had talked about it on their last visit for Boone's birthday. As Boone listened, he could see his mom was excited to share the good news with him. He began to feel guilty for his embarrassment over his mom calling to him.

Then she told him what the news was. He was even more embarrassed when he heard what she had to say. Grandpa and

Grandma wanted him, just him, to go with them on a camping trip for three nights and four days to one of his favorite places. They were going to Tatanka State Park for their 45th wedding anniversary and they wanted him to help them celebrate it.

Tatanka happened to be one of Boone's favorite places too. Grandpa and Grandma and his parents had taken him there many times. He knew the trails well. Lake Tatanka, a large lake in the park, was one of his favorite places to fish.

Wow! he thought, *three nights and four days in Tatanka, what a great way to begin the summer!*

Then raw guilt struck his heart. He bowed his head. His shoulders slumped. His mom's smile turned into a frown.

"Why the sour face, Boone?" she asked softly. "I thought Tatanka was one of your favorite places."

He didn't answer her; instead, he looked at her eyes.

"Mom, I need to apologize to you."

His mom's frown turned puzzled.

"Mom, I felt you embarrassed me. I was embarrassed that you were my mother. Now I know why you called my name for the whole neighborhood to hear. You did have good news! Great news! I am sorry mom. You are always good to me. Will you forgive me?"

He knew the answer as he spoke the last word. Though he was 13, the hug his mother gave him was a big relief.

Then she said, "I forgive you, Boone. I love you too."

When she kissed the top of his right ear, he squirmed out of her hug. Forgiveness he wanted, but a kiss was not on his want list. He looked at his mom. Her eyes were sparkling, and he thought he saw tears.

Turning stubborn again, Boone said, "Mom, I needed your forgiveness, not sloppy kisses."

His mother just reached out and mussed the hair on top of his head. "Sorry," she said, "guess I got carried away. Boone, do you want the details of Grandpa and Grandma's trip to Tatanka State Park now?"

He snapped alert. How could he forget? "Yes, mom, please, I do." He walked into the kitchen and sat down at the counter.

She began with when they were going. "Their anniversary is June 6, in four days. They plan to go after church on Sunday in order to be at the park for the 4 p.m. check in. They said they would pick you up on the way. Grandpa told me to tell you to pack your fishing gear and your hiking boots."

Boone was just about to ask why when mom explained.

"He said they were also planning to do some hiking on the trails during the cool times of the day. He said they would fish from shore on Tatanka. He wanted you to know he planned to fish at night for walleyes."

Boone knew what that meant without his mom telling him. He interrupted his mother with, "And Grandpa said to bring my lighted bobber, didn't he?"

His mom looked surprised, "Why, yes, he did!" She smiled. "Oh," she added, "he said, 'don't forget your rain gear, it can rain at Tatanka this time of year.'"

Boone was nodding as he walked by his mother, patted her shoulder and walked to his room. He tossed his school-worn backpack on the floor in the corner. He did not plan to pick it up any time soon. Then he remembered he had just added clutter to the floor. He opened his closet door, picked up the backpack and hung it on the closet hook. Realizing he was hungry, his about-face turned him back to the kitchen. His mom was still there.

On the kitchen table he saw two freshly-frosted cinnamon rolls. The frosting was melting down the sides. His mom had even warmed them in the microwave. A cold glass of milk sat beside the plate. Boone forgot himself and walked quickly to his mother, threw his arms around her neck and squeezed. Two words came from his mouth, "Thanks, Mom!"

With two cinnamon rolls and a tall cold glass of milk settling his after-school hunger, Boone returned to his room and took his camping backpack out of his closet. His rain gear went in first. He did not plan to use it, he was sure it would not rain. Within five minutes he had socks, underwear, extra t-shirts, two pairs of jeans and a sweatshirt rolled and neatly arranged in the backpack.

As he lifted the backpack off the bed, he decided to add a long-sleeved t-shirt he could layer under the sweatshirt. He knew the air temperature after sunset would cool quickly. He wanted to be warm for after dark when walleye move in to shore for baitfish.

He headed to the storage locker his dad kept in the garage for the fishing rods during the summer. It did not take him long to remove his walleye and panfish rods. He set them in the corner of the garage, leaving the rod covers on to protect them. They were ready for Grandpa and Grandma to come.

He reached for his tackle bag, unzipped the bag and removed the walleye box. He checked his crankbaits. He thought about fishing with live bait, and decided he would be sure he had leader material for setup of Lindy rigs. He checked the weights and the swivels. He had enough.

He reached into the side pocket and found his lighted bobber. He checked to see if it lit. It did not.

He was headed for the laundry room where his parents also stored the supply of new batteries when his mother called, "Boone, time for dinner!"

It was then Boone felt his stomach growl. *Wow*, he thought, *I just had my after-school snack. Where did time go?* He did a quick pivot and headed for the kitchen.

With his head down, thinking about batteries for the bobber, he did not see his dad leaning against the doorway to the kitchen. He walked into his father. "Uff," the air went out of his lungs. Boone felt his dad's arms go around him.

"Hey, son," he said, "great to see you. What are you thinking so hard about?"

Boone's head snapped up.

"Oh, hi, Dad. Batteries, Dad, I am thinking about batteries. My lighted bobber does not work. Do we have any like these?" He showed his father the two small round batteries that fit in the bobber. His head 'no' told Boone they did not.

"We'll need to buy new ones. These are not very common, but I am sure we can find replacements," he said. "Why do you need batteries for the lighted bobber?"

Boone looked at his father with a bit of surprise on his face.

"Haven't you heard, Dad? Grandpa and Grandma are taking me with them for their 45th wedding anniversary! I'm sure we'll be fishing in lake Tatanka...after dark too. Dad, if we fish at the fishing pier, we can float a bait after dark. The lighted bobber will work well."

Boone's dad looked at him a moment, then nodded his head and gave Boone a pat on the back. Boone knew they would get the batteries.

Two days later Boone sat in the back seat of Grandpa's pickup. He couldn't stop his foot from tapping on the floor mat. He politely answered Grandma's questions. Actually, he was happy to, but he was couldn't wait to get to the park. He had thought about nothing else since the last day of school when he learned he would go with his grandparents. He thought about how his lighted bobber with new batteries would show in the water when he fished from the pier.

He thought about fishing from one of Grandpa's two kayaks. He tried to remember – did Grandpa say he was going to bring them along? He sure hoped so. When he got in the pickup, he had forgotten to look if they were in the back. He took a quick glance backward. They were there!

His imagination kicked into hyperdrive. He imagined himself floating near the lily pads on the edges of Tatanka with spinner baits. He knew Tatanka had extra-size largemouth bass. He could just imagine what hooking into one would be like, sitting in a kayak.

The last thing he couldn't stop thinking about was drift fishing in the kayak. He knew it was one of Grandpa's favorite ways to fish. Many times in the last two days he had imagined the two of them on drift patterns across one of Tatanka's sand bars.

There was something else he thought a lot about – Grandma's special meals. Grandma was great at pancakes; actually, Grandma was great at anything food. He hoped she'd brought some fresh cookies. He didn't want to be rude and ask her, he decided to wait and see. He liked surprises. The biggest surprise of the summer so far was going to Tatanka State Park with his grandparents. He leaned back in the seat. His foot stopped tapping. Boone was enjoying this. The power check had already begun, in the back seat of Grandpa's pickup.

"Thank you, God, show me your power on this trip."

The campsite Grandpa and Grandma selected was near the shore of Tatanka. Boone found himself staring at the blue waters of the big lake. He greatly enjoyed watching the ripples lit with sparkling sunshine. Boone's teacher had once called them water diamonds. This was a school detail Boone remembered. He thought of the words each time he saw sunlight sparkling on water. He thought "beautiful" was a perfect word to describe it.

The three of them ate their evening meal on a picnic table at the campsite. Grandma seemed to know just what Boone would like. She made the meal in aluminum foil. Grandpa put the packages onto the hot coals of the campfire he started while Grandma put the meals together. The hamburger and vegetables always came out tender, juicy, and flavored with a tinge of smoke. Boone's mouth watered just looking at them. They were as delicious as they looked. Cleanup was easy. Boone washed the glasses and forks while Grandma sat in the shade reading the Bible she had brought along.

While he was cleaning, a subject he had not thought of during the meal came to his mind. It was fishing. He knew the pier was only a block from the campsite they were at. He knew with dusk coming something that never failed to cause him endless wonder was happening. Walleyes were moving into the shallows of Tatanka. But he didn't dare ask – he was Grandpa and Grandma's guest. He decided watching the lake would be almost as good as fishing.

He pulled a camping chair next to Grandma's. Boone wasn't surprised to hear the scrape of another chair on the sandy campsite earth. He looked away from the lake to see Grandpa settling into a chair next to his grandmother's. As his gaze lingered, he noticed Grandpa reach for Grandma's hand. Boone looked away with a smile. He found great comfort in how his Grandpa and Grandma loved each other.

He shifted his gaze towards the middle of Tatanka to the black loon silhouettes floating over the deep clear water. Boone forgot about fishing. Birds fascinated him almost as much as fishing. Quietly he went into the camper, found his backpack and dug into it for his binoculars. Closing the camper door as soundlessly as possible he made his way back to his chair. He could see the details of the loon's feathers with his binoculars.

He became completely focused on the loons. He timed the length of their dives with his watch. His skin tingled when one of the loons made a long trembling yodel. The call echoed far back into the hills around Tatanka. Boone's heart was full. He closed his eyes. Though he was just 13, he had learned that every good and perfect gift comes from God. He thanked God for the perfect gift of the cry of a loon on a big lake. Maybe that's why he jumped when he heard Grandpa call his name.

"Boone, the walleyes are in around the pier. Would you like to greet them with a leech on a hook?"

Minutes later, after a hug and a thank you to his grandma for the great meal, Boone and his grandpa were on the way to night fishing. As he turned on his lighted bobber, Boone said another brief prayer of thanks to God. This day had been absolutely wonderful in every way. He had a feeling there'd be walleyes for dinner the next day. Minutes later he knew it as he watched grandpa reel in the first fish...it was a keeper.

Boone was thinking about taking his grandparents on a hike on the Hoka trail in the park. *Hoka* was the Lakota name for *badger.* They were once common in the park. Boone hoped they might see a badger's den on the trail.

When his lighted bobber disappeared, Boone's thoughts about the Hoka trail vanished with it. He would ask them tomorrow.

"Fish on!" Boone called to his grandpa.

Chapter 10

Lost

"They will speak of the glorious spendor of your majesty,
and I will meditate on your wonderful works."
— Psalm 145:5

Boone and his grandpa began fishing an hour before sunset. They caught four walleyes in the "slot," the size limit in which walleyes may be kept. Four fish were enough for a generous fish meal the next evening, with a frozen package for Boone to take home for his parents. It was late when the two of them got the fish cleaned and packaged for an overnight in the camper refrigerator. Grandma had already gone to bed. Being thoughtful, the two had laid out their pajamas before leaving to fish so they wouldn't wake her when they came back.

Before fishing, Boone had rolled out his sleeping bag in the back-packing tent he had set up next to Grandpa and Grandma's camper. With little sound and no talking, the two fishing partners were soon asleep. Grandma had already gotten a head start.

Boone's last thoughts before sleep overcame his active mind were that taking a hike with Grandpa and Grandma would be something he would enjoy after breakfast. The Hoka trail was his goal.

He thought about the badger dens he had seen along the trail a year ago. The black and gray fur of a badger was the last thought he had before sleep put his quick brain into rest mode.

Boone was still asleep when Grandma had her family-favorite pancakes started. Grandpa walked out to Boone's tent and unzipped the tent door. Boone's head popped up at the sound. He saw Grandpa bending to look into the tent. He smiled at the man he loved as much as he loved his own father.

"Good morning, Grandpa."

"Good morning, fishing buddy. Time for breakfast," Grandpa answered.

"I'll be there after a trip to the bathroom, Grandpa."

Boone was out of the tent before his grandpa had stepped into the camper. He returned to the camper just as his grandmother was flipping over the first pancake. It was golden brown, with a mouth-watering aroma that sat Boone down at his place in anticipation...his grandma was a pancake expert! The three family members reached for each other's hands and bowed their heads in prayer.

Grandpa spoke, "Would you thank God for our breakfast, Boone?"

Taking a deep breath, Boone paused. Grandpa or Grandma were the ones who prayed, he was the one who listened. But Grandpa had asked him to pray. He took another deep breath.

He opened his eyes in a brief blink. Grandpa and Grandma had their heads bowed; they were waiting. Boone decided to be brief.

"God, we thank you for the beauty of the earth you have made. Thank you for your protection overnight. Thank you for teaching Grandma to make delicious pancakes. Bless our breakfast and our day. I pray this in Jesus name, amen."

Boone did not realize how God's blessing on the day would be needed later on.

"I'll take a pancake, please, Grandma," he said with a smile. His smile broadened when Boone noticed the maple syrup Grandma had set on the table. It was his favorite. His grandfather had made it. The syrup came from the maple trees in Grandpa's woods. He collected the sap and boiled it down to syrup in his shed behind the house. Boone knew not all people liked maple syrup. He was one of the ones who did.

"Grandpa, would you please pass the syrup?"

Boone's mouth watered. Grandma's pancakes with maple syrup were one of his favorite breakfast food combinations. A small spread of butter melted on the hot pancake just before Boone poured over the homemade maple syrup.

After his first two pancakes and half a glass of milk, Boone found himself thinking about the day at Tatanka Park. He remembered his thoughts the night before about hiking the Hoka trail. Remembering not to talk with food in his mouth and not to interrupt, he waited for his chance to speak. He decided to ask Grandma first about his hike idea.

"Grandma, could we hike the Hoka trail after breakfast?" Wanting to insure she said yes, Boone added something he thought would convince her to say yes. "I'll do the dishes." He did not feel any guilt, he was not bribing. He wanted to help his Grandma. Hiking the Hoka with a chance to see a badger or a den was Boone's goal.

Grandma smiled. Grandpa smiled. She reached over and gently tousled Boone's hair. Boone always felt a tingle of joy when Grandma touched his head. But he was surprised to hear his grandmother say, "We want to go on a hike with you, no bribery is needed. But, since you offered to do the dishes, you can!"

Boone had the breakfast dishes done quickly and carefully. He remembered his grandmother's instructions to rinse the dishes in hot water; then let them drain and dry in the air. He found himself feeling thankful for hot water from the faucet of the camper. As he finished the last dish and set it to drain, he turned to look at Grandpa and Grandma sitting around the small camper table. They still had their coffee cups. He glanced at the coffee pot. It still had coffee in it.

He could say, "Are you done with your coffee yet?" Or, he could be still and join them. He decided to sit down with his grandparents. As he sat, he noticed they had a map of Tatanka Park spread on the table. He remembered his dad's advice before he left with Grandpa and Grandma.

He said, "Boone, be a listener when you are with Grandpa and Grandma. They are wise. You can learn from them."

Boone heard them talking about the Hoka. Grandma was telling his grandpa that she thought the trail was too long for her. She said, "Four miles are more hiking than I want to do at once."

Boone winced inside. She sounded like she did not want to go. His grandpa's response was not encouraging either.

He said, "We could always hike a mile or so and then turn around and hike back. It is surprising what you see on a trail when you hike it in reverse. Boone, what do you think?"

Boone forgot his father's wise advice. Hadn't Grandpa asked for his advice? He was going to give them his great knowledge. "All about Boone" kicked in. He did not realize his pride was going to create a problem for them all very soon. With enthusiasm in his voice, Boone began.

"How about a shortcut, Grandma? We can hike the Hoka for about a mile and then cut through the woods on a deer trail here. We'll pick up the road to Tatanka Campground when we come out." It should only be about two miles."

Boone traced his finger down the Hoka, through the woods where he proposed a shortcut and back on the campground road.

Grandpa responded with caution. "I don't know about a shortcut, Boone. We are not familiar with the woods off the trail in that area. We could get turned around."

Now Boone's pride swelled again. Grandpa was hinting that he might get them lost. *Not me*, he thought.

"Grandpa, I have been through this part of the woods before on a school trip. I know my way."

Boone was pleased when his grandma said, "I am sure Boone knows where to go, Grandpa. We can follow him. This sounds like a good way to see new places in the park."

Grandpa opened his mouth to speak, then closed it. As Boone looked at his face, he thought he saw a twinkle in Grandpa's eye. Then Grandpa said, "OK, we'll follow Boone."

While Boone was pleased they would not be backtracking and that they would see the woods as they cut across to the campground road, he was a bit disappointed that their hike would be shorter than he had hoped.

He did not say anything. He did not want his grandmother to become tired. Later that evening he was proud of his grandmother's stamina.

Boone liked to travel light. He grabbed his water bottle when he saw Grandpa take two bottles for him and Grandma to share. Boone left his compass in his backpack in his tent. In fact, he left all his survival gear in his tent.

Within five minutes they were headed for the trail link to the Hoka. Boone was excited. He imagined seeing a living badger, or if not, then its tracks or den. He had never seen one in his life. He knew there would be many other surprises on the Hoka. His steps were filled with energy.

He suddenly decided to be bold and ask Grandpa and Grandma to do something for him. He said, "Could we use hand signals instead of talking when we are on the trail? We'll see more animals that way."

Grandma smiled and nodded. Grandpa smiled and put two thumbs up. Boone's response was a pat on his Grandma and Grandpa's backs. Boone's heart was full. He was on a wild trail with two of the people he loved greatly. He was sure they would see unexpected things and Boone definitely liked nature surprises.

The soil of Tatanka Park was sandy. In places, large rocks stabbed their way out of the trail. Boone savored the land like a good burger fresh from the grill. He liked the sand because it always left a track record of the animals that walked across it. The rocks were often covered with gray or green and sometimes orange lichen. Just the trail would keep his attention. Yet, Boone balanced his views of the trail with steady inspection of the woods on either side. Often, he looked deeper into the woods for the frozen tan silhouette of a white-tailed deer. He was continually using his ears to pick out sounds of animal and bird activity around them. His dad and grandpa had been his teachers. Boone listened and learned from both.

Boone felt the southeast breeze on his cheek. *Just right*, he thought, *comfortable, neither cold or hot*. The campground link trail soon came to the Hoka. It was Boone who suggested they take the trail northward. It would lead them along the east shore of Tatanka lake with views Boone had never seen before, even when he had come on a field trip with his class at school. Glimpses of sun-sparkled water through leafy tree branches caught his eyes.

He did not gaze long at the sparkling water of Lake Tatanka. His eyes and mind were fixed on the possible sighting of a badger. As they walked in quiet companionship, Boone thought of what he knew about the badger. He remembered they were mammals. Then the word "carnivore" came to mind. But he knew that besides living on a diet of gophers – both pocket and ground squirrels – as well as mice and voles, badgers ate insects, eggs, reptiles and even roots of plants. That would actually make them omnivores. Their food came from the habitat they lived in, usually large grassy prairies.

Boone knew it was unusual for badgers to live in Tatanka Park. He also knew that while the park did have many acres with tree cover, there were enough large grassy areas for badgers to live. Boone thought the black, white and gray pattern of the badger's fur was beautiful. Then he remembered that the badger was an outstanding digging machine. He was thinking they were mostly nocturnal when they walked into the first open prairie of the Hoka trail. He realized the chance of seeing one was unlikely. A few steps further, Boone spotted the large and fresh pile of earth first and pointed to it.

His grandparents stopped. Boone looked at them. They both motioned for him to go forward. Boone was pleased and surprised. They wanted him to investigate first. One could approach more quietly than three.

Boone smiled at the two people he knew had made sacrifices for him to come along. Then he nodded at them and took his first step, his eyes fixed on the fresh animal-made hole in the earth. Careful where he put his feet, he kept his eyes on the den and walked with slow, soundless steps. As he watched, he saw a shower of fresh earth fly up and out of what seemed to be a badger-sized hole. He stopped and signaled to his grandparents, who signaled thumbs up. They had seen it too. In that moment, Boone realized he might have a rare chance of really seeing a live North American badger.

He decided to make himself smaller. He crouched down, kneeling on the trail, and froze. There was movement at the den entrance. It was not flying dirt. It was black, gray and white. Boone blinked. He was eye to eye with a powerful earth-moving mammal, the badger. Boone's eyes went to its shiny fur. The light southeast breeze made each hair shimmer. He could see puffs of wind moving badger fur.

Wow, this is beautiful, he thought. Boone had read about the badger's power. He saw it now. He also witnessed a boldness. The badger saw him, Boone knew it. But rather than quickly hiding in the tunnel it was burrowing, it turned and faced him. Boone watched as the badger's nose worked back and forth pulling in

his scent. Boone did not move, not even a twitch or a blink of his eyes. What seemed like a minute or more was only seconds, and then the badger vanished into the burrow. Boone knew he would not see it again.

Slowly and quietly, he rose. He signaled for his grandparents to join him. Soundlessly they walked to him. Together they walked up to the den, which Boone guessed was less than five feet off the trail. Boone knew that was accurate. His grandmother's hiking stick was a bit more than four feet long. When Boone borrowed it to measure the distance by laying the stick on the trail's edge and the other end to the burrow, the end of the stick came to the center of the burrow hole.

The three of them stood silent before the burrow. Boone had also read that badgers are clean mammals and that they kept the insides of their burrows clean, another reason he liked badgers.

Several moments later, he heard himself sigh. He took a breath and whispered to his grand-parents, "We can go now."

Grandpa's response was a soft, "OK."

Boone did not notice the small prairie-covered hill or the blooming blazing star that grew among the big bluestem. He did not feel the south wind on his cheek. He never noticed the deer tracks just beyond the badger's fresh burrow. His mind was still on the badger. How beautiful it was when the wind made puffs on its shiny black, gray and white fur. He remembered how its fur shone in the sunlight. He remembered its black, wet nose working out his scent as it watched him through badger eyes. He remembered that the animal had showed no fear, only a quiet strength.

As he walked, he remembered God's part in this amazing event. Boone believed seeing the badger was a gift from God. He couldn't control this wild powerful animal, but God could.

It made sense to Boone. If you had power to create things, had all power, knew all things and could be everywhere present, well, God could bring the badger out when Boone arrived. Boone silently thanked God for the gift of the badger.

Five minutes down the trail, the trio came to a trail map sign. Boone's confidence was high. He glanced at the map and confirmed the shortcut he thought they should take. He then traced the route with his finger as his grandparents watched. Both nodded in agreement. They would follow Boone as he led them. Boone was sure they would be on the camp road headed back to camp just before lunch. After a short hike that took them into the next wooded area, the three left the security of the trail. Boone soon picked up a deer trail that led west toward the Tatanka Campground road.

Boone took a quick glance at his grandma. Was she tired? He saw the smile on her face, her step was strong. Boone looked beyond his grandma to Grandpa. Grandpa was watching him. He winked.

Boone turned and took his next steps. He decided they should follow the deer trail as long as it headed west. As Boone gazed around them, he was certain they would soon come to the campground road, but before they did he was enjoying the beauty of the forest around them.

Boone found delight in finding large trees. There were many, most of them maple. *Grandpa could gather lots of maple sap here*, he thought. Boone also found enjoyment in the numerous mushrooms and fungus he observed growing on the forest floor or the trunks of aspen or ash trees.

The first alarm went off when Boone stepped out onto a hiking trail. He had been expecting the campground road, not a trail. No trail should have been between them and the road they planned to hike back to.

When Grandpa and Grandma stepped out of the woods onto the trail, Boone suggested they take a drink of water and rest for a time.

His grandpa said, "Which way, Boone?"

The second alarm went off. Boone did not know. His pride and false confidence prevented him from recognizing the truth. He was lost.

With more confidence than he felt, Boone answered, "We'll go to the right."

It was then Boone noticed it felt warm and he was thirsty. He was glad for his water as he took another drink. He saw Grandpa and Grandma were sharing their last water bottle. He noticed the bottle was already half empty. He glanced at his. How did it become half empty?

Walking another 10 minutes brought them to an open area, which looked entirely new. The trail made a fork.

Again, Grandpa asked, "Which way Boone?"

With a stutter, Boone looked left then right and said, "Let's stay on the left. Uuh, Grandpa, I think I'm lost."

Boone immediately felt better. He had admitted the truth. He had pushed away his pride.

Grandpa responded by saying, "Let's pray. Grandma, Boone, take my hands." Grandpa prayed, "'Lord, you know where we are. We are never lost with you. But we have lost our way. We need your help. Calm our hearts, enable us to think clearly.' Now, Boone you said left, let's see if this brings us to the road."

This time Grandpa led. He gently took Grandma's hand and led her toward the trees along the trail that went left. Boone, his pride tarnished, followed them. When they got through the trees, they saw a gravel road. The road to the campground was tarred. Boone was even more confused.

A feeling of panic struck him. They were really lost! He was hot. He glanced at his water bottle, only a few swallows remained. He knew Grandpa had asked God to guide them, and protect them. But he was still scared.

Then he remembered Grandma. He glanced at her. There was still a smile on her face. She noticed Boone looking at her. She put her hand on his shoulder.

"Boone, we'll be OK. Now we know this trail is not the right way. We are closer to finding our way now. Do you think we should turn around and go back the way we came?"

Boone sighed. Grandma's touch was comforting, it calmed him. But all he could do was nod his "yes."

How he wished he had taken his survival pack with him. His compass would help right now. Slowly he turned. He looked up. Grandpa and Grandma were waiting.

Grandpa spoke now. "Boone, I have become turned around more than once here at Tatanka park. We'll go back the way we came. Something will look familiar soon."

Boone's smile was small, but it was a smile. *OK*, he thought to himself, *let's go back.* He led the way. He began to pray. Over and over, he repeated, "God help us, God help us."

Ten minutes later they were back to the place where they first came to the trail. They continued on. Boone's water bottle hung empty on his belt loop. Grandpa and Grandma had emptied theirs too. It seemed to Boone they had been on the trail for hours. He walked. He prayed as he walked. The fear began to go away. It was replaced by embarrassment. He had promised his grandparents he knew the way. They had put their trust in him. He had failed them. His prayer changed. "Forgive me, God, forgive me, God," he repeated again and again.

He looked ahead. Suddenly he knew where they were. Still a long walk back, but he knew. With growing excitement, he turned to his grandparents. "I know where we are! We have come to the horse camp! There will be water to drink here too."

A few steps later they walked into the grassy area of the horse camp. Boone knew it was the horse camp. But as he looked around, he had no idea where the road leading to the camp road was. He did know they could stop at the nearest water hydrant and fill their water bottles for a drink. The first gulps were marvelous. Then Boone felt hungry. He shared his feeling with Grandma.

"I'm hungry, Grandma. Your pancakes were delicious. I think I could eat six of them right now."

Grandma responded with a peek at her watch. "Boone, what time is it do you think?" Boone's guess was 10:30 a.m.

He was shocked when Grandma responded with, "It's 12:00 noon and lunch time, Boone my boy."

Boone sat down. He was even more embarrassed. He knew he needed to apologize. He looked at Grandpa and Grandma.

"I'm sorry I had so much pride. I'm sorry I've gotten us lost. Grandma, I'm sorry you have had to walk so far. This is all my fault. I should have listened to Grandpa." Slowly his grandparents walked to where he sat. In a moment both were sitting next to him, one on each side. Boone felt their arms go around him. He felt his grandma's head lean against his temple.

"Boone," she whispered, "I forgive you. Besides, this has turned into a memorable adventure. And Boone, I don't feel tired – well, maybe a little, but I am fine."

He felt Grandpa squeeze his shoulder gently, "Fishing buddy, let's find the road to the camp road and walk home for lunch."

Filled with a grateful heart for love from these two people, Boone stretched out his arms and hugged them both. Before he could stop himself, he heard himself blurt out, "I love you both!"

A surprise greeted the three of them as they trudged up the hill on the horse camp road. They came to a lady who had just loaded her horse into her trailer. She was just preparing to leave. After Grandma explained what had happened, the lady generously offered them a ride back to Tatanka campground.

Ten minutes later, with many thanks to the lady who gave them a ride, they were back at Grandpa and Grandma's camper. As they walked the short block back to the camper, Boone said what was on his mind. "Grandpa and Grandma, I think that lady was really an angel."

Without a word, Grandma prepared large peanut butter and grape jelly sandwiches and poured three cold glasses of milk. Between mouthfuls of sandwich, Boone apologized again.

His grandparents both said, "Boone we love you," and Grandpa, his eyes twinkling, said, "Thanks for the adventure."

Chapter 11

The Unexpected
Happened

*"Now to him who is able to do immeasurably more than all we ask
or imagine, according to his power that is at work within us..."*
— Ephesians 3:20

The camping trip with Grandpa and Grandma to Tatanka
Park turned on a switch in Boone's heart. It changed his
thinking for the rest of his life. The memory of being lost would
come back to him when he did not expect it. When he shared his
feelings with his grandpa one day, Grandpa's answer astonished
him.

"Boone, God is using our getting lost to teach you. God's
Holy Spirit is reminding you of how you felt and what you
thought. He is using it to build you into the man He wants you
to be someday. Listen, and obey."

When he heard Grandpa's explanation the first time, Boone
had listened. Boone was thankful that somehow God was using
that time of fear and humiliation at Tatanka to teach him. He
found that life was certainly not all about him like he once
thought. With his parents, Boone found he did not want to be
stubborn with them. He was careful to choose his words and not
speak in anger. He even felt that keeping his room picked up and
clean was something he could do because he loved his mom.

He was surprised and pleased to find the old "all about me" Boone didn't show up much anymore. When he did, Boone preferred the respectful, polite and responsible Boone a lot more. He found he enjoyed pleasing his parents. He still found it hard to think that getting lost at Tatanka could make such a change in his thinking, or that God had used it to teach him. Whatever the reason, Boone decided he wasn't going back to acting the way he had been.

His parents soon noticed too. A delightful peace settled over Boone's family that even his brother and sister noticed. It came up one sunny summer morning. Boone was feeling grumpy. His brother and sister had just emptied the box of cereal that happened to be his favorite too. As Boone picked up the empty box and shook it, anger came. This was unfair. They took all of the rest of the cereal and left none for him, and they knew he liked this cereal!

Boone opened his mouth. He was about to break the peace of his family. He did not care, this was too much. They were selfish.

Then his brother said something that stopped Boone's anger. "Boone, I'm sorry. I forgot how much you like this cereal. Hold on, I saw mom put a new box in the cereal cupboard yesterday."

Boone's mouth dropped open in shock as his brother went to the cupboard and brought out a new, full box and set it on the table in front of him. A smile spread across his face. All he could say was a surprised, "Thank you." As he took his first bite, he thought how thankful he was to have kept his mouth shut.

That evening he found himself thanking God for setting a guard on his tongue. He realized he did not want to become angry or be disrespectful. It felt good. No, it was better than good. Maybe getting lost had helped. Then Boone realized God is in control of all things. He liked the feeling of gratefulness.

But the very next morning, things were difficult. Boone had it again. He had experienced this feeling before. He knew what he needed to fix it too. The urge to go fishing was on his mind.

He knew from experience that after a few days he would find himself thinking about water, specifically water in a lake. For a while he knew he could be content with imagining the waves splashing on shore and the sparkle of light from the sun on the water. He liked when water looked like diamonds. He also knew, because he had experienced it many times before, that before even two days passed he would find himself thinking about what swam in the water – fish. It had been more than a few days. He wanted to go fishing.

He needed to go fishing. He said the words he found himself repeating often to his dad, "Can we go fishing today?"

When he said them, he knew the answer would be no. His family was busy. His dad sometimes was the most busy of all. He just felt better when he said those words. He needed another power check.

This time things were different. All of Boone's family would be traveling to his grandpa and grandma's place. They lived near two lakes. He could fish there. Boone found it was hard to concentrate on other things when he needed to go fishing.

His best power checks came when he was fishing. He thought about fishing before breakfast. Sometimes it was the first thing that came to mind when he woke up. He thought about fishing after breakfast. He thought about it before lunch, after lunch and most of the time every evening. When he needed to go fishing, it made him restless. It made him walk around the house, and outside the house – it was hard to sit still.

When he went fishing, he felt better. Or perhaps it was fishing provided him with a way to do a power check. Whatever, Boone had it again. He had experienced this feeling before. He knew what he needed to fix it too.

He couldn't explain it. The thought of unseen fish in water sometimes was all he could think of. Where were the fish? Did this lake have fish, or that one? How many were there? Always he wondered where the biggest fish was. He could imagine himself fishing for them. He wondered if they would bite on artificial bait or live bait; minnows perhaps would be better than nightcrawlers. He could even imagine how it would feel to catch them. Yes, Boone had fishing fever, he had it bad.

He knew at his grandparents he could do something about it. He knew he could ask his grandpa, "Can we go fishing soon?"

He knew his grandpa would say, "Yes." Boone smiled; he knew his grandpa had fishing fever too.

When they arrived at Grandpa and Grandma's, Boone knew he had to wait before he asked. He answered his grandparent's questions. He was polite at the evening meal and talked about school and his part-time job doing yard work for their neighbors. They asked him about his grades. He told the truth. He could have done better in two classes. Inside he was bursting to ask the most important question in his life at the time, "Can we go fishing, Grandpa?" Though he knew it might be too soon, he asked when Grandma passed the dessert, his favorite oatmeal cookies with chocolate chips.

"Grandpa, can we go fishing before sunset?"

Boone was puzzled when he saw his grandfather's face with a slightly unhappy look on it.

Grandpa said, "Yes, we can, but the boat is not available now. The motor doesn't work right. But we can fish from shore.

Boone's face got an unhappy look on it. He wanted to fish the lake in the boat. But he quickly changed his mind. He had waited a long time to go fishing. Lake, shore, it did not matter if he had the chance to catch a fish.

As they got their fishing gear together from Grandpa's old tool shed, Boone saw the shovel hanging from a nail.

"Grandpa, I think we should bring some worms for bait." Grandpa's answer was to get an empty old-fashioned red coffee can from his workbench.

"We can put them in here," he said.

This was another part of fishing Boone enjoyed, digging in the earth in Grandpa and Grandma's garden for earthworms. The smell of moist earth and the quick curling of exposed earthworms was almost as good as fishing. The worms could not get away like a fish, and sometimes an earth clod held a jumbo fat nightcrawler two or three times bigger than an earthworm.

Another part of fishing Boone looked forward to was spending time with his grandfather. Since they would not be using his boat, they could walk to the channel and fish just a block from the house. They talked about fishing. They had decided to bring a pail to keep keep the fish in if they caught any large enough for a meal. Boone liked eating freshly-caught fish almost as much as he delighted in catching them. Grandpa reminded him of something he had not thought of. The small mouth bass had to be returned immediately to the water. Grandpa then made him feel better when he told him that they would take a picture first.

At the channel, they walked under the bridge where they would fish. It was quiet there; the sounds of traffic above were dim.

Boone remembered another reason why he enjoyed fishing so much, it was the excitement of the unexpected. He looked into the clear water as Grandpa got one of the fishing poles ready to use.

He asked Boone what they should use as a hook, and they decided on a small chartreuse jig. The between-bright-yellow-and-green color always showed up in clear water and usually drew fish. They decided to add a rubber worm tail for an extra attraction. When the worm was added, they were ready. Boone took a deep breath delighted to be able to drop this special bait into the water. He was ready for the unexpected. Would it be a sunfish, an aggressive bass, or possibly a tough, scrapping northern? Boone cast into the clear flowing water. He was fishing at last. He could not stop smiling.

He could see fish in the water below him and he decided to drop his bait in front of one. He watched with delight as the small sunfish swam to the bait and gulped it into its mouth. Boone lifted the rod tip and the battle was on. It was short. The sunfish was little, but beautiful.

Boone called out to Grandpa, "I think it's a bluegill, see the black tips on the ends of the gills?"

His grandpa agreed and Boone carefully unhooked the little fish and released it back to the channel. It could grow larger.

Boone then caught two smallmouth bass, but they were only palm-size and he released them too. A few minutes later a sunfish almost as large as his hand took the worm. They decided to keep this fish and Grandpa put water in the bucket to keep it alive.

Boone was so busy catching fish and having fun at the same time that he did not notice what his grandpa was doing. Grandpa had not caught any fish, but was experimenting with different lures. Boone did not see when Grandpa put on a silver spinner with a bucktail covering the treble hook at the end. He did not see Grandpa cast it out into the middle of the channel. He was not watching when Grandpa let the bucktail spinner sink in the current while the silver spinner flashed like a minnow. He did not see Grandpa pull the rod back as he felt something stop the bait at the bottom. Grandpa told him later he thought he had snagged a rock. But then it moved. Rocks don't move. It was 6:30 p.m.

Boone became aware of what Grandpa was doing when he heard his name.

"Boone, you should land this fish; here, take the rod."

Boone quickly set his fishing pole down, careful not to damage it on the rocks. He was by Grandpa's side a few seconds later. As he took the pole and felt the weight, his first thought was Grandpa really has snagged a rock. Then the rod bent and he felt the heavy pull. The drag slowly clicked as line left the spool. This was a fish. This was a *big* fish.

A brief thought flew through Boone's mind: *this was certainly unexpected.*

He glanced at Grandpa. He was watching Boone with a smile on his face.

Softly Grandpa said, "Keep the rod tip up, keep steady pressure on the line, we will need to tire this fish out to land it. This fish seems too big for us to power it in, the line is not heavy enough, it will break. Boone, this may take awhile."

Boone took a deep breath and smiled. This was much more than what he came for. But his left arm was already getting tired.

Grandpa spoke again, "Boone, let's set the time we hooked this fish at 6:30 p.m. It's 6:35 now."

Boone said, "Five minutes, just five minutes and I am already tired of fighting this fish. Wow, I never expected this either!"

Boone and Grandpa settled in for a long battle. They discussed what kind of fish was on the treble hook at the other end of the line. At first, they thought a northern pike or perhaps a large musky. Both were found in the lake. Grandpa discarded both ideas at the same time he remembered there was no steel leader to protect the tough but fragile monofilament line from northern or muskie teeth.

Grandpa said, "I think it is a sturgeon."

Boone heard the mystery in his voice. He felt the big powerful fish pull slowly deeper. This was a new fishing episode in Boone's young life. Boone was surprised by it. The strength of the big fish amazed him. When he tried pulling it up, it would not move.

Grandpa began softly calling out the elapsed time. Fifteen minutes after hooking the fish, Boone told his grandfather he was switching hands on the rod. His left arm felt done in. He switched hands, all the while keeping the pressure on the line and the tip of the rod up. The two talked softly. It seemed wise. Perhaps loud sounds would cause the giant to struggle and break the line. Perhaps it was the nearness to a large fish that quieted them. From the beginning, Grandpa had been coaching Boone, and he was eager to listen. Landing the fish became more important as the minutes flowed by. Grandpa suggested pulling up and reeling in when there was some slack line. Boone lifted slowly but the fish did not move. He could gain nothing.

"Grandpa, I am afraid the line will break," he said.

Grandpa softly spoke one word, "OK."

So, Boone held on.

He heard Grandpa say, "It's been 30 minutes since we hooked this fish."

To Boone it seemed longer. He switched hands again even though both arms ached. They both agreed that every few moments he would try to lift the fish. Their strategy was to gradually tire it. The talked about the best place to bring the fish to the edge of the channel where they could attempt to land it. There was no easy place, just uneven rocks. Grandpa said out loud, "I wish we had a net." A few minutes later he would discover his net would have been too small.

Boone kept the pressure on. He would gain a few feet, only to lose it minutes later when the fish settled deeper near the bottom in the fast-moving current. Not until much later did grandfather and grandson realize the strength it took the fish to dive deeper with two forces pulling it up and back: Boone on the line, and the strong river current.

Another unexpected thing happened at 7:15 p.m. Boone's mother, older brother and sister came to where the marathon wrestling match between boy and fish was going on. There was a family campfire for their family at 8:30 p.m. Boone's whole family and his grandparents were going. His mother came to get them. But she did not interrupt when she saw what Boone was doing. Now there were four others watching Boone strive against the strength of the big fish. It was quiet. The others let Boone concentrate. All eyes were on the water.

Grandpa softly called out the time: "It's 7:25. Boone, you've had this fish on for 55 minutes."

The final unexpected thing happened quickly. The big fish came up, Boone took in slack line furiously. Then they all saw it. Later, they agreed the fish was more than three feet long. It rolled at the edge of the channel, just below the rock shore. Still, no one moved. They could not land the fish, the shore edge was too steep and rocky. Then the fish took back the line Boone had furiously recovered. The drag clicked rapidly as monofilament stripped off the reel. The fish did not stop when it got to the bottom. It rolled and moved downstream.

Then Boone said the words they had dreaded hearing the most, "It broke the line."

Grandpa watched as Boone reeled in and was surprised to see the buck-tailed spinner still attached. In some unexplained way the heavy sturgeon had thrown the hook. It was free.

Grandpa looked again at his watch. Disappointment clear in his voice he said, "Boone you fought that fish for 56 minutes."

A connection to great mystery in nature was over. Boone had just experienced a fishing memory many who fish never have in a life time.

Boone glanced at his watch and looked at his mother, it was time to go home. It seemed like they had just come. They talked about the sturgeon on the walk home. Their main objective was to be truthful about the size of the fish. Though Boone and his grandfather had not landed the fish and they did not touch it, they had a gift most anglers who connect with a large fish never have: they saw it. In fact, Boone had four witnesses: Grandpa, his mom, his brother and sister. They laid a tape measure on the grass of Grandpa's lawn to better estimate the length of the fish. They agreed it was over 45 inches. Later they found that, according to sturgeon length and weight charts, a 45-inch sturgeon would weigh 27 pounds.

His mother said, "I have never seen a fish that big before."

Boone thought to himself, *this is why fishing is exciting, sometimes the unexpected does happen.* He could not wait to go again.

He had felt God's power in that big strong fish. On the walk home to Grandpa and Grandma's house, the thought of homework when school began, taking out the garbage, and for sure obeying his parents would be his regular priorities.

Yes, he thought to himself as he walked alongside his grandfather, *I need power checks.*

His grandfather just put a hand on his shoulder and with a smile said, "Help me get the campfire ready."

Chapter 12

The Ball Game

"As iron sharpens iron, so one man sharpens another."
— Proverbs 27:17

oone's weekend at Grandpa and Grandma's was much
better than he expected. The unexpected gigantic fish
yesterday, the family campfire and tubing after church behind
Grandpa's boat were great fun. Fixing the motor with Grandpa
before going to the lake was something Boone found extra
satisfaction from. He had helped his grandfather remove the
four spark plugs from the motor. Then he helped put the four
new plugs into the plug holes in the motor, then tighten them.
When they started the motor at the lake, it worked like new.
Boone found the whole experience to be exceptionally satisfying.

Yes, it was a good day. Boone had spent much of the
afternoon on the water, literally. He was separated from the
water by three layers: nylon, plastic and a lot of air...a tubing
tube. Boone hadn't thought of fishing once. Well, once as the
tube straightened out behind the boat and he wasn't hanging on
with all his strength. He saw a quiet spot at the edge of the far
shore and wondered if a bass would be in the newly-blooming
lily pads. Otherwise, he was on the tube. When he got off to

let others take a turn, he enjoyed their attempts to stay on the doughnut moving at 25 to 30 miles an hour eight inches off the water. Yes, it had been a great afternoon, but summer days are long in the north country where Boone lived. Now for some reason, he found himself thinking about baseball. He was surprised. Usually, there were fish on his mind.

If you put in order the favorite things in Boone's life right now, there were three. Fishing was first. Baseball (or the sport in season) was second, and anything else that brought him to the water was third.

He'd been on or near the lake all afternoon. Before the evening meal was through, Boone asked his grandpa the latest question now filling his mind, "Grandpa, could we play a baseball game?"

Boone found Grandpa wasn't as easy to convince about this as he was about going fishing. He was old. Baseball meant running. Sometimes running hurt. But that was mostly afterward. So, Grandpa stalled.

"We don't have enough players. I've been outside all afternoon."

Boone was ready for that one, "We'll play the two-player game."

Grandpa was curious, "What's the two-player game?"

Boone had this one. "It's easy, Grandpa. This version of baseball is only for two players."

But Grandpa was still determined. It showed in his answer, "That doesn't sound like it could ever work."

Now Boone launched the full "I'll convince you, Grandpa" attack. Boone had Grandpa ready to play in a few seconds.

"Grandpa, it's exercise, you know how healthy exercise is."

Boone got the whiffle ball plastic bat. He looked in the sports equipment box his grandma had organized in their garage. A tennis ball caught his eye. He picked it up. They would play with a tennis ball.

When he got outside, Grandpa was pulling weeds in the garden. Boone wondered how that could be interesting. Boone liked vegetables, but he did not get the attraction to a garden. Grandpa had it.

He called, "Grandpa, I have the bat and ball."

He watched as his grandpa slowly stood. Boone thought, *I can beat Grandpa in a race, easy.*

The end of the sidewalk behind the house would be first base. They dropped an ice cream pail cover on the grass for second. The post for bluebird house at the corner of the garden would be third. Home would be the general place where they stood to bat. They would not worry about touching home, they would be honest with each other, gentlemen's agreement to be fair.

The diamond was ready. The two players were ready. Boone said, "Grandpa, you be up first."

Grandpa took a few practice swings. To Boone, he seemed a bit stiff. Boone began to think, *Maybe this game won't be so much fun.* He decided to play just to humor his grandpa, because after all, it was his idea. That's when Grandpa started the play-by-play color commentary. Boone almost let his mouth hang open in surprise.

"Folks, it's the top of the first inning and the first playoff game for the World Series. It's Old Navy meeting the Yellow Jackets for a final series of the season. These two teams have played each other even during the season. Each team has beaten the other six times and won six times in the 12-game regular season series. The Yellow Jackets lead-off batter tonight is 'Old Buzzard.' He looks slow. He seems to swing his bat slow, but the Old Navy pitcher knows he can hit."

What? He'd never heard Grandpa talk like this. Then Boone was curious.

"Why are you the Yellow Jackets, Grandpa?"

Grandpa answered quickly, "It's my yellow shirt."

Boone noticed Grandpa's yellow shirt.

"Then why am I Old Navy?" was Boone's curious comeback.

"Look at your shirt," was all Grandpa said.

Boone did not need to look down to remember that he was wearing his Old Navy shirt.

Boone was stunned. Where did Grandpa get all that chatter? Maybe this was going to be fun. Just listening to Grandpa call the game would be entertaining.

He threw the first pitch. Grandpa swung too late and the ball sailed behind him to the imaginary backstop. It was Grandpa who suggested they have only two outs. It was Boone who determined there would be no "ghost runner" Both of them wanted the two-player game to have action and be fast paced.

Grandpa struck out – twice. Boone thought he'd change that when he got up to bat. But Grandpa struck him out twice.

His color comment was, "Folks, it is early in the game, but the Old Navy and Yellow Jacket pitchers look extra sharp tonight, don't be surprised if we find ourselves with a no-hitter going...for both pitchers."

Boone chuckled to himself. *A no-hitter. Where does Grandpa get this stuff?* he thought.

Boone began to enjoy this two-player game. He especially enjoyed the "color commentary." As the second inning began and Boone readied himself for the first pitch, he heard his grandpa say, "Fans, it is early in the game but it is clear to see the Old Navy pitcher is nervous about facing Yellow Jacket batters at the top of the second inning. He threw a lot of pitches in the first inning. I see confidence in the eyes of the Yellow Jacket batter. It is clear he has stepped into the batter's box to hit the ball. This could be an interesting inning."

Boone did not enjoy this comment from Grandpa. He stared intently at Grandpa. He took a deep breath and focused on striking Grandpa out. He did in just seven pitches. There was a big smile on his face when he picked up the bat for his turn in the bottom of the second.

Before Grandpa threw the first pitch, Boone suddenly heard him say, "Time out!"

Boone was momentarily confused. Time out? What for? There were only two players, Grandpa had the ball, he looked fine. Why time out?

Then he heard Grandpa say, "Here comes the Yellow Jackets pitching coach to the mound."

Boone watched as Grandpa put his hand to his mouth and made mumbling sounds like he was talking with the coach so no one else could hear or see. Boone almost laughed out loud again. The pitching coach!? Where does Grandpa get these ideas, he wondered? His thoughts were interrupted by Grandpa's next colorful comment.

"It looks like the Yellow Jackets are going to force this Old Navy batter to hit the ball on the ground. It seems they are looking for an easy ground out. But if that's not what they talked about, then the Yellow Jacket pitcher will be throwing heat for a strikeout."

Boone took a quick breath and stood straighter. He was not striking out and he planned to hit a long fly ball. But he struck out twice.

Grandpa's color comment: "The Yellow Jacket's pitcher is on fire!"

Now Boone thought his grandpa was getting boastful.

By the top of the 5th inning, Boone thought his grandpa was right about a no-hitter. As the inning began, the score was 0-0. Grandpa was at it again.

"Fans, this game has the makings for a classic playoff game by two evenly matched teams. Have you ever seen such controlled pitching? Both pitchers have displayed complete control of the game. They throw strikes. I do not think I've seen two pitchers more relaxed. This is a real pitcher's duel."

Boone had to agree. Old Navy batters (that was him) could not get a hit, and neither could the Yellow Jacket batters (that was Grandpa).

With no hits after six innings, Boone wondered if there would be any score in the game. Maybe they would need to just end the game. Then it was his turn to bat in the bottom of the 7th inning. Grandpa revealed what he was thinking as he added his color commentary.

"Baseball fans, this game is quickly becoming one for the record books. We've had six complete innings with not one hit and no errors. Fans you are watching a highly unusual game. Both pitchers have no hitters going as the Old Navy leadoff batter steps up to the plate. Folks, this batter is nervous!"

I absolutely am not nervous, Boone thought to himself.

When Grandpa threw the first pitch, Boone hit it over the garden. It rolled all the way to Grandpa's wood pile. Boone whooped his way to first and whooped some more when he reached second and Grandpa was just bending to pick up the ball. Boone jumped on the imaginary home base to show Grandpa he was there. The no hitter was over.

"I scored, Grandpa!" Boone whooped inside this time.

Grandpa's response was more color commentary. "Baseball fans, this game just got more exciting. A home run late in the game! The pressure will be on the Old Navy pitcher when he faces the Yellow Jackets next inning. But can the Yellow Jacket pitcher get out of this sudden jam? Seems to me he's nervous now!"

This time Boone laughed out loud, and Grandpa struck him out again with three pitches.

"It's the top of the 8th inning, folks. We've got a new ballgame. Old Navy has just punched in a run with a towering home run over the garden. The Yellow Jackets have had extra quiet bats for the entire game. It will take some clutch hitting now – can they do it?"

Boone's response was to pound his glove and stomp on the imaginary pitcher's rubber on the imaginary pitcher's mound. He stared in at Grandpa and threw a strike, Grandpa swung and missed. Boone struck him out five pitches later. Boone got excited – just three more outs and "Old Navy" would win!

He slapped his glove, pulled the ball out and threw the next pitch. Whack! Grandpa drilled the ball to the same spot Boone's homer went to. It seemed as Boone began to chase the ball down that it had rolled even closer to the wood pile. He heard Grandpa whoop. When he heard the second whoop, he knew Grandpa was on his way to third.

I'll catch him before he gets home, Boone thought.

Grandpa was only on his way to third. Boone got close. He stretched out to tag Grandpa out just as Grandpa whooped and stomped on home. He ran faster than Boone thought he could.

"What a ball game!" Grandpa shouted.

Boone smiled. Slowly he walked back to the pitcher's mound. He turned and threw the ball right down the middle. Grandpa swung and drove the ball right back to Boone, who threw his glove up to protect his face. To his amazement, the ball stayed in his glove. While Boone was amazed at what had just happened, he heard Grandpa's excited voice.

"Did you see that folks? What a ball game! You just witnessed a baseball highlight of the week! What reflexes! What a catch! That ball would have rolled all the way to the garage, maybe even curved into right field for another run for the Yellow Jackets. This is baseball at its best."

When the 9th inning ended, the score was still tied. Grandpa really got into the idea of a tie game after nine innings.

"Baseball fans, you've gotten your money's worth for this game. You've witnessed a pitching duel with two fine pitchers going toe to toe. You've seen a defensive play that was unbelievable. For sure this is the best of baseball.

Boone didn't need to think about it. This *was* a good game, he agreed with the color commentator as he walked to the pitcher's mound to start the 10th inning. Then he proceeded to get Grandpa to hit a little rolling grounder toward first. To his surprise, he struck Grandpa out on three pitches for the second out.

When he stepped up to bat in the bottom of the 10th, Boone was down to six strikes. He did not need five of them. Grandpa held off on the color comments and threw the first pitch of the bottom of the 10th. Boone drilled it. This time the ball sailed over the apple tree on the west side of the garden and landed in the neighbor's yard.

Grandpa didn't chase the ball, he whooped. "Can you believe it, folks? The Old Navy player dug deep and nailed the first pitch. It's a walk-off home run! What a beautiful hit! Old Navy wins!"

Boone thought, *this was almost better than fishing.*

Smiling, he walked over to Grandpa and held out his hand to shake it. In his heart, Boone thanked God for the man who had just given him a gift much more than just a ball game.

Chapter 13

I've Got One!

"Trust in the LORD with all your heart and lean not on your own
understanding; in all your ways acknowledge him,
and he will make your paths straight."
— Proverbs 3:5-6

Yes, summer was one of Boone's favorite times. His other favorites were fall, winter and spring. Truthfully, Boone liked every season. Summer heat and thunderstorms, swimming in the lake and fishing made the warm season go quickly.

But leaves changing color and falling with cool evenings and morning frost were fall events Boone always looked forward to. Fishing could be great in fall. But fishing in winter was one of Boone's favorites, especially after discovering spearing last winter. Then there was spring. Boone found immense joy in watching migrating birds returning, trees in bloom with new green leaves following. He found a special delight in watching sunlight sparkle on ice-free water. When it came to seasons, Boone did not have a favorite, he liked them all and looked forward to observing the changes that came with each.

One thing Boone especially enjoyed about summer was the week he could be at Bible Camp. Everything about camp pleased him. The counselors, learning about the Bible, campfires, the food – and yes, he could fish at camp – all these were enjoyable.

This year he was especially pleased that his neighbor and friend, Logan, was able to go to camp for the first time with him. Together they enjoyed the entire week. The packed camp schedule made each day seem shorter than normal and time went by quickly.

On the way home from camp, Logan surprised Boone with these words, "You know Boone, Bible Camp screams of a Creator." Boone agreed completely.

Now Boone found the two of them at his grandparents for the evening. His family was on the way home with a stop at Grandpa and Grandma's first. Boone was pleased and surprised to find his younger cousin Weston visiting Grandpa and Grandma. He always enjoyed Weston's full-of-life personality.

He knew Grandpa had the boat working well now. He decided to ask the question he was known to ask often, "Could we go fishing tonight after our meal?"

Boone thought he would get a 'yes' answer. He knew the boat was working. He knew Grandpa liked to fish as much as he did. There was even a final bonus, his dad could go. Boone was sure he would hear a 'yes,' and that was exactly what Grandpa replied.

"We can do that Boone. It will be a very nice evening to be on the water, too. We'll go after dinner. There will be plenty of daylight too, our summer evenings are light until after 9:00 p.m."

Boone did an in-his-head backflip. He heard himself silently shout, "Yeeha!"

Grandpa's boat was big, comfortable and fast. He liked that the boat had two fish finders and a big trolling motor on the bow. He liked that you could walk around in it and stand on the bow deck to cast in front of the boat. He was planning his fishing strategy already. With evening coming he would cast spinner baits from the bow towards the shore and shallow water. Boone could already imagine the feel of a muscular largemouth bass tearing line off the spool. His imagination threw in a few twisting bass jumps into the air. The image was just right. Thinking about fishing was almost as good as the real thing...but not quite.

Grandma's supper was delicious. Eating was one of Boone's favorite things to do. He seemed to be always hungry, and Grandma seemed to know just how to prepare food. One of her specialties was the spaghetti and meat sauce she served them all for supper. Boone ate one plateful and started on a second when he remembered fishing. His grandpa had already pushed away from the table and was talking with his older brother, Noah. While Noah was excited to go fishing, Boone knew his brother would rather be playing baseball or any sport instead.

Boone looked at his dad across the table, he made signs with his hands like he was fishing and then tapped his watch. Boone's dad got the hint. When Grandpa had finished his words with Noah, he asked, "Grandpa, Boone wants to know when we will be going fishing?"

Grandpa jumped out of his chair. "Oh, fishing! I forgot!" I'll get ready right now."

Like that, Grandpa was out the door. Boone heard him start his pickup and then he heard it back out of the garage. Boone went to grab his rod and reel and tackle bag. He helped his friend Logan get his rod and tackle bag – they'd both had their equipment at Bible Camp. Noah and cousin Weston would use Grandpa's fishing gear.

When he got to the shed where Grandpa stored his boat, he overheard his dad and grandpa talking about where they should go. He heard Grandpa say if more time fishing is what they wanted, they should go to Ironwood Lake – but Lake Anna would be good also, yet farther away with less time to fish.

Boone's dad answered with a question. He asked, "On which lake will we catch more fish?"

Grandpa quickly answered, "Anna."

Boone was proud of his dad – he knew what boys wanted... fish on!

Boone remembered Lake Anna from a trip they had taken last summer. It was a beautiful lake. One thing Boone especially liked about Lake Anna was that much of its shoreline was undeveloped and natural. Boone did not mind when people built their lake homes, but he thought lakes with natural shoreline and less development were more interesting.

Lake Anna had a lot of natural shoreline to enjoy. Leafy green tree limbs reaching to the shore with dark silent woods behind brought a mystery to the lake that Boone liked. Sometimes fishing great blue herons, and even a solitary eagle, would perch in the dead limbs of cottonwood trees near shore.

Boone thought back to his first trip to Lake Anna when they had seen majestic eagles perched together on a tall tree near shore. He remembered their white heads and tails brilliant in the morning sunlight. He already had good memories of Lake Anna. Now he was thinking about fish as he climbed into the back seat of his grandpa's pickup to sit next to Logan.

His cousin Weston had already buckled into the seat behind his grandpa. Boone could tell Weston was excited too. He had just asked Logan what kind of fish he liked to catch most. Boone was curious and listened. He had fished with his friend Logan in their home state where there were different fish.

He was surprised when Logan's answer was, "Sunfish." While Boone was surprised and puzzled over the answer, Logan added, "I really like how a big one fights."

Boone chuckled when Weston asked, "What's a sunfish?"

Logan gave a quick answer, "It's a round fish with a small mouth that fights like crazy."

Boone did not know that all four of the boys in Grandpa's pickup would have a much better idea of what a sunfish was before the evening fishing trip was over.

To a boy anxious to wet a line, it seemed time dragged on and on before Grandpa said, "Everyone 'ucklebuck'."

Boone always laughed at Grandpa's way of reminding everyone to wear their seatbelt. When he was younger, he would laugh out loud. Now, as a teenager for a few months, he kept his laugh inside. "Uklebuck" was Grandpa's backward way of saying buckle up. To Boone it seemed Grandpa would use that word forever. Weston did not keep his feelings inside. He laughed out loud and loudly said, "Grandpa, you mean buckle up, right?"

Grandpa never turned around and in the same voice repeated, "Everybody-ucklebuck!"

Boone knew Weston understood when he said, "OK, Grandpa, I'm buckled."

Then Boone realized they were moving. Finally! They were on the way to Lake Anna and fishing in Grandpa's big boat.

The next day Boone could not remember what he and Logan talked about with Weston. He did remember Weston being full of questions, which he and Logan took turns answering. He also remembered one question Noah asked as he sat on the front seat between his dad and grandpa. Later, Boone was glad Noah had asked it.

After they had been driving for what seemed like too long to Boone, Noah asked, "When will we get there, Grandpa?

Boone was delighted when Grandpa's answer was, "We are past the halfway point. We'll be there soon."

When they turned onto the short gravel drive to the Lake Anna public access, Boone remembered another thing from his first visit to Lake Anna last summer. He liked the lake access. It was so quiet. Today, there was only a car and a pickup with an empty boat trailer. They wouldn't have to wait to get on the lake.

Then Boone discovered the reason why someone had driven a car with no boat trailer to the access. There was a couple with their dog, a chocolate lab. He didn't know why, but he noticed the wedding band on the man's finger as he tossed an orange training dummy into Lake Anna for the dog to retrieve. Perhaps it was the golden gleam on the man's finger.

Although fishing was overpowering every other idea in Boone's mind, seeing the wedding ring brought a quick realization: *I like knowing there is a ring. It tells me they are married.* Boone realized that the marriages of his parents and grandparents had made his life happier. Then, snap! Thoughts of fishing quickly pushed their way into his mind.

Just as quickly, he noticed the sunfish swimming under the dock. One of them looked oversized. He couldn't wait to get on the water, so he asked his dad if they could take out the fishing rods they had stored in the rod locker of the boat.

His dad just answered, "No." Then he explained, "We'll be on the water sooner if we wait."

A short time later, Noah, Weston and Logan joined Boone, his dad and grandpa on the boat. Grandpa started the motor and backed away from the dock. Boone felt himself relax as he leaned back on one of two jump seats on the back deck of the boat. They were finally on the water.

He began to examine the lake. He always did this when he first came to a lake. He looked at the water nearest shore on his right, then his left. He liked to compare and predict which shore would hold more fish. He never got a chance to this time.

He had just begun searching the east shore when the motor revved and Boone felt his head jerk back. Grandpa had opened the motor up! They seemed to be flying across the water. Boone sat back and let the wind blow through his hair, glad he had taken his cap off before the wind could blow it into the lake. He gazed up at the blue sky and decided to simply enjoy the beautiful evening.

In what seemed like three seconds later, he heard Grandpa say, "Let's fish here by these lily pads."

Before he could look down, he heard the rod locker being opened, and then Grandpa passed fishing poles to Noah and Weston.

"Drop your lines over the side boys," he said.

Boone jerked to attention. They were fishing! He didn't even have his rod out of the locker. He bumped into Logan as he leaned forward to take his rod out.

He was apologizing to Logan when he heard Weston call out excitedly, "I've got one!"

Boone was distracted again. He looked to the stern of the boat where Weston was and saw him holding a fairly large sunfish high in the air. Grandpa had to help Weston settle down a little to help him take his fish off. Boone turned again to reach into the rod locker and bumped into his dad, who was stepping to the bow to help his brother Noah take the fish he had caught off the hook.

Boone apologized again. This time he kept his focus and got his rod and reel out. He had not even got his line in the water yet! Shutting out the excitement around him, he snapped a small jig on his hook. He would not bother to tie it on, he needed to start fishing. He quickly threaded a tiny cylindrical sparkle bait through his hook and dropped the lure and bait over the side. As he did, he watched the line drop slowly into the water next to the boat. Out of the corner of his eye he saw a passably respectable-sized sunfish swim toward his bait from under the boat.

Then he heard Weston shout, "I've got one!"

He turned his head to the stern of the boat again and watched as Weston reeled in another sunfish bigger than the first one. Boone forgot his own line until he felt a strong tug. He quickly glanced down in time to see the fish swimming away and swallowing the sparkly bait.

Out loud he exclaimed, "I missed one!"

As he reeled in to rebait his hook, he told himself to focus and fish. He did. A few moments later it was Boone who said, "I've got one!"

He smiled as he reeled in a wiggling, bullheaded sunfish who tried to swim sideways into deep water before Boone wrestled it to the surface. He was disappointed when he saw the size of the fish. Though his dad and grandpa had the final say on putting the fish in the live-well, Boone already knew it was too small.

He reached for the fish to take it off the hook and was rewarded with a sharp prick in his finger from the spines on the dorsal fin of the fish.

He couldn't help it, he yelped out loud, "Ouch!"

The word came out before he had a chance to think about being strong and grown up.

His dad leaned in and said, "If you want, I'll take it off for you, Boone."

He was threading a new sparkly bait on his hook when the words he was coming to expect came again. "I've got one!"

Boone was not surprised to see Logan reel up another sunfish. As Boone looked at the fish, Logan said out loud what Boone was thinking, "It's too small, we'll put it back in the lake."

Boone felt another tug. He quickly glanced down, just in time to see another sunfish swim away with his bait in its mouth. Boone could not help himself – out loud he exclaimed, "Pay attention!"

Everyone in the boat turned their heads and looked at him. Boone felt his face go red. For the third time he apologized. "I'm sorry, everyone, I was talking to myself about focusing on fishing, not on what everyone else is doing."

Boone felt painfully foolish. He realized the "about me Boone" was back.

He felt a hand on his shoulder.

"Thank you, Boone, that took courage. It is hard to admit when we are wrong." Grandpa was smiling at him.

Boone felt the red begin to disappear. He smiled back at Grandpa and took a deep breath.

Still looking at Grandpa, he said, "I guess it would be good if I stopped thinking about myself. Maybe I'd catch more fish?"

Grandpa patted his should and then gave it a gentle squeeze. "I think that will work, Boone. Now, bait up and catch one!"

While Boone was baiting his hook again the words, "I've got one!" came loud and clear. It was Weston with another fish.

Boone never looked, but he heard Grandpa say, "This one can go in the live-well."

Boone almost turned his head, but stopped as he saw movement below him. A dark fish had moved just below his sparkling bait. He watched motionless as the fish seemed to gulp the bait and hook into its mouth. Boone set the hook. His rod bent. It was a good fish. *Oh, this was fun*, Boone thought, *I've got one!*

As he reeled the fish to the surface, he realized that it was not a sunfish. The dark spotted sides contrasted with silvery spots were different. He saw Grandpa looking too.

Grandpa spoke with excitement and loudly, "Boone, you've hooked a crappie, beautiful! This one goes in the live-well."

They caught fish after fish for the next two hours. After a few more fish, all sunfish, Boone decided to snap on the spinner bait Grandpa offered him. He followed Grandpa's advice and threw it in toward shore. As he jigged the bait back toward the boat, the bait stopped moving. Boone set the hook again. He watched with delight as his rod bent again.

"Fish on!" he said with a smile. The bass kept working its way back to the weed bed where it had been suspended in wait for an unwary baitfish. Boone kept the pressure on and soon boated a largemouth bass.

Dad patted his shoulder. "Nice fish, Boone," he said with a smile, "but this one needs to grow some more."

Boone lipped the bass himself and took out the hook. He held the fish upright just below the surface and watched as it began to move its gills to breath. When it began to move its tail, Boone released his hold on its lip. It gave a quick flip of its tail and quickly swam into deeper water.

The words "I've got one!" were repeated many times during those memorable two hours on the water. Between the four boys, Boone's dad estimated there were 70-80 fish hooked and brought into the boat. Boone couldn't believe it! He'd never seen so many fish caught at once. Before they moved off the lake there were 12 large sunfish in Grandpa's live-well. Boone boated two more bass on the spinner bait, then decided to catch sunfish like the others. His brother Noah, the one who liked sports better, caught enough fish for Boone to think maybe Noah would like fishing after this.

On the way back to the public access in the fading light of sunset, Boone went back to thinking. This time, not about where the fish were. This time he was thinking about two good things.

First, he'd learned a life lesson on Lake Anna. He'd discovered that life is better lived when he stopped thinking about himself. "It's not about me," Boone whispered to himself.

The second good thing? He loved his family. His dad had been patient and encouraging, Grandpa too. Weston's excitement turned out to be memorable. These were two good things.

Boone glanced ahead – there was just enough time to thank God for this trip. Eyes open, mind on God, Boone said, "Thank you, Lord, for teaching me. Strengthen me to remember life is not about me. Oh, Lord, thank you too for the wonderful gift of family, for Dad, Noah, Weston, Grandpa, and especially for good friends like Logan."

Boone saw the boat access coming quickly, and as Grandpa slowed the motor to approach the dock, Boone closed his prayer by saying, "Thank you, God, for fish!" He couldn't wait to go again.

Chapter 14

Fishing on "Soft" Water

"...honor your father and mother, and 'love your neighbor as yourself.'"
— Matthew 19:19

The evening of fishing on Lake Anna had not faded from Boone's memory when the next opportunity to fish came. Boone did not expect it. His next fishing trip came as a surprise. Boone had to thank Pastor Andrew for this.

Just after breakfast a few days after the Lake Anna Trip, his grandpa texted him. Grandpa told him Pastor Andrew wanted to take the two of them fishing. Was Boone interested?

His dad heard Boone's shout from the garage where he was washing the car.

"Yes!!!"

Then Boone remembered he needed to text his answer to Grandpa. He could hardly wait for an answer. It did not take long.

Grandpa responded right away with the words, "Be ready tomorrow 7:30 a.m. Pastor Andrew wants to take us "soft" water fishing."

Boone ran to the garage where he knew his dad was cleaning the car. He was afraid to ask, since he knew he had just gone fishing the week before. What would Dad say? Boone had not asked for permission first. He had simply answered Grandpa with the answer he wanted: "Yes, I can go."

So, with doubt in his voice, Boone began to ask his dad. "Dad, Grandpa just texted me..."

His dad interrupted, "Is that what the shouting in the kitchen was about? Then, yes."

Boone was confused. Had his dad said, "Yes?"

Boone explained again, "Dad, Grandpa asked me to go fishing with Pastor Andrew and I said 'yes,' but I never asked you first."

"You can go...we think you might need another 'Power Check,'" his dad quickly added.

Boone was stunned. "But Dad, I never asked you first. I'm sorry, I got so excited that Grandpa asked me to go fishing I forgot to ask you."

"Your grandpa asked first," his dad responded. "He told me he would be texting you this morning. It's OK, your mom and I already know and we approve...you are set to go."

Boone saw the smile on his dad's face as he reached out to hug his neck. "Thank you, Dad! I love you."

His dad reached out to give Boone a gentle thump on the back. "Mr. Boone, I love you back." His hand thumped on thin air. He looked up to see Boone headed into the house. "That boy does have fishing fever," he said shaking his head while a smile formed on his face.

Inside, Boone bounded downstairs to the furnace room where he and his dad stored their fishing gear. He took two of his favorite rod and reel combinations from the holder on the wall. He reached onto the shelf by the back wall and slid his hand through the handles of his tackle bag.

One other thought came to mind. Spinner baits – did he still have that white one with the silver flashers? Quickly, he reached into the pocket on the right end of the bag. Yes, there were three colors of spinner baits in the sandwich bag he kept them in. One of them was white with the silver flashers that triggered a fish bite.

He looked at his watch. Boone still wore a watch. He found freedom in not carrying his cell phone in his pocket all the time. Recently he had made a decision to use his phone only to contact others. He did not use it to access the internet. He found he actually had more time for things he truly enjoyed. One of them was fishing.

It was only mid-morning! Grandpa and Pastor Andrew would not come for nearly another 19 hours. What was he going to do? Then what Grandpa said in his text came back to him. Pastor Andrew wants to take us "soft" water fishing. Boone was instantly confused. "Soft" water? What did Pastor Andrew mean? He knew it would be difficult for him to concentrate on other things now. All he could think about was fish swimming... and maybe chasing that white spinner bait with silver flashers. And what was "soft" water fishing?

But it seemed like a short while before he was brushing his teeth for bed. The next thing he heard was his cell phone alarm chime. Boone was amazed. He had slept all night!

He did not linger in bed. He was ready for Grandpa and Pastor Andrew at 7:00 a.m. Ready, that meant standing in front of the garage door with his fishing gear next to him. With a soft south wind touching his cheek, he began the watch. The watch... looking for Pastor Andrew's old red pickup to drive up the street.

That first day of "soft water" fishing with Pastor Andrew and Grandpa stuck in Boone's memory for a long time afterward. After greeting Boone, Pastor Andrew asked him a question he could not answer at first.

Pastor Andrew asked, "What do you like better, soft or hard water fishing?"

Boone did not understand. *Soft? Hard? Water was water.* Then he spoke his thoughts aloud to Pastor Andrew, "Isn't water...well, isn't water...water?"

Pastor Andrew said, "Boone, there are two kinds of water for a fisherman...in winter it is hard, there is ice on it. In summer it is soft...no ice."

Boone laughed and then a smile stuck to his face. He thought about hard and soft water until he noticed they were at the lake.

"What lake is this?" Boone had never seen it before. He knew they were driving on a different road. He never thought there was a lake nearby.

Pastor Andrew gave a quick answer: "It's Loon."

While Boone began to contemplate this fact, he heard the pickup doors open and close. He never noticed Grandpa and Pastor Andrew at the shore. They were turning over the fishing boat. Boone jumped when he realized he was all alone in the truck.

"Hey! Wait for me!"

Standing with his gear in hand, Boone let his eyes roam around the shores of Loon Lake. He could see no houses, no cabins...no docks and not any other boats.

"Wow!" Boone was amazed. "Why aren't there any houses or boats here?"

Pastor Andrew looked up. "It's a private lake, Boone."

Boone looked at the lake again, this time with delight. "Oh, boy..." He didn't say another word.

When the men had it ready, Boone looked at the boat. It was tiny, there were dents in it. One of the oars had a chunk out of the end. And what did Pastor Andrew have for a motor? Was that an electric trolling motor? The boat did have three seats. There were three fishermen.

Pastor Andrew called to Boone, "Mr. Boone, you've got the front seat. You run our anchor. Can you do it?"

The men had pushed the boat into the water by the time Boone walked up to it. He put his life jacket on and watched while his grandpa and Pastor Andrew pushed the boat out further and got in. They had their life jackets on, they always wore them. Boone was glad no one had to remind him to put his life jacket on.

Holding his gear, Boone stood frozen, thinking about the tiny boat, the little motor and the private lake, and fishing in the last month of summer before school started.

He heard a voice, it was his grandpa. "Boone, did you want to get in? Let's go fishing!"

Boone jumped again. Then he took two quick steps and put his gear in the front of the boat and left room for himself to get in. That done, he pushed the boat into the lake.

If you asked, Boone could tell you the details of that first fishing trip on Loon Lake. The tiny boat leaked...just a little. Whenever Pastor Andrew asked Boone to anchor, he would

lean forward to drop it over the side, and that slight increase of pressure on the bow of the boat forced water into the boat through the patch...just a little. The electric trolling motor worked wonderfully...until the battery died. Then Grandpa rowed. The oars worked too, even with a chunk out of the tip on one.

Then there was the fishing. What fishing it was! Soft water fishing was just as good as hard water! The three fishermen had caught fish to put in the freezer. Next to fishing, eating a meal of fish was one of Boone's favorite things.

Boone could not put in words what his time in a boat fishing with two men who loved God meant for him. He knew he wanted to go fishing with them again. He truly enjoyed fishing, but time with those men was something he found as good as fishing.

That evening he remembered something from the Bible his mother and father had told him months ago. He remembered how he had understood they were speaking to him because they loved him. They reminded him what the Bible said about giving honor to your father and mother and loving your neighbor as you love yourself. He thought Grandpa and Pastor Andrew were worthy of all the honor he could give them.

Chapter 15

The Wreck

"When he thunders, the waters in the heavens roar;
he makes clouds rise from the ends of the earth. He sends lightning
with the rain and brings out the wind from his storehouses."
— Jeremiah 10:13

The fish Boone and Grandpa caught with Pastor Andrew were soon eaten. Grandpa had reminded Boone more than once that the "best fish were fresh fish." That meant eat them soon after they were caught. Boone felt especially fortunate. He was able to eat two fresh fish meals. One at home with his family, the other at Grandpa and Grandma's. For some reason Boone could not explain, Grandma's fish meals always tasted just a little better than those at home. Then, just like that, there were no more frozen fish at Boone's house or at Grandpa and Grandma's.

In the early days of summer, Boone had found there were many things to keep busy with. During the school year, which ended two months ago, Boone had discovered another thing he found as enjoyable as fishing. It was reading. That summer Boone's hands were often occupied with holding the current book he was reading.

His favorite summer reading place was outside, near the family garden and by the wood pile. Boone didn't need a chair – he sat on the grass and leaned against the pile of wood. If he felt too cool, he sat in the sun, too warm, he sat in the shade on the other side of the pile.

Keeping his room picked up and in order had become a habit. Controlling his tongue, well, that was more difficult, but he was learning to ask God for help to "*set a guard on his tongue.*" Boone knew it was working. His parents noticed the difference. When it came to Power Checks...well, Boone still needed them.

Power Checks refreshed his attitude, they filled him with a peace he could not find any other way. They enabled him to control his tongue. Boone even felt less selfish and more satisfied with everything after a Power Check. But after Grandpa and Pastor Andrew introduced him to Loon Lake, Boone could not stay satisfied with long periods of time between Power Checks.

The next day after the first trip to Loon as Pastor Andrew called it, Boone's dad found Boone's fishing gear spread out on the downstairs workbench in the furnace room. Besides being the place where the furnace was located, it was the place where the fishing gear was kept. It was also where household projects were completed on the workbench.

His dad had a project – sharpening the chain on his chainsaw. But he found Boone's fishing gear laying on the workbench. In fact, it covered the whole top. His also noticed another thing that made him smile. All of the fishing gear was in order. The rods and reels were lined up. Boone's line clipper lay alongside them, and next in line were three different colored spinner baits.

When Boone's dad went to ask Boone to move things off of the workbench so he could use it, he could not resist asking why all the fishing gear was lined up on the bench.

Boone's response was logical, and very believable. "Dad, I just can't keep Loon Lake off my mind. I was planning for the next trip to fish there. When I can lay out the gear it helps me plan. Dad, I think I enjoy my fishing gear like you enjoy keeping your chainsaw working well." It was a long speech for the usually quiet Boone.

After Boone had cleared away his gear so his dad could work on the bench, Boone's dad called Grandpa instead of working on the chainsaw.

When Grandpa heard how much Boone was thinking about another trip to Loon Lake, his response was, "I'll give Pastor Andrew a call after we hang up. And this could be considered an emergency – we do not have any fresh fish in our freezer."

Grandpa did not waste words or time when it concerned fishing. The fishing trip was set for the next day. The fishing gear was spread out on the workbench as soon as Dad had finished his work on the chain saw. This time Boone organized things for a real fishing trip, not a fantasy one.

The unexpected happened during the night. Because Boone was usually unable to sleep as soundly before a fishing trip, he heard and saw the storm. He woke first because of lightning flashing in the distance. The flashes which blinked on his eyelids gave him a clue of the approaching storm. When the storm was over the house, Boone watched as the rain fell and the wind whipped the branches of the trees beyond his window. He was not afraid and the storm passed over in minutes.

Boone was thankful he fell asleep for the few hours remaining before wakeup. Fishing time came at 7:30 a.m. To Boone this seemed to be Grandpa's and Pastor Andrew's regular time. The trip to Loon felt like it passed more quickly too. Boone enjoyed listening to the two men share thoughts and ideas. They both seemed to talk about God more than anything else...yet fishing was never far from either man's mind. Boone shared his opinions when they began to discuss where they would fish first on the lake.

Boone was thinking about which color spinner bait to use when he heard Pastor Andrew exclaim, "Why is that oar leaning against the fence post? It's supposed to be under the boat."

Boone was completely in the moment then. As they drove down the slight incline to the lake, Boone was alarmed to hear Grandpa say, "The boat is missing!"

When he could peer around the seat in front of him, Boone saw that the little boat was not in its place in the tall grass. There was a bare spot left by the boat, and one oar...but no boat.

During the next half hour, all three wanna-be fishermen walked along the tall grass near the shore where the boat was supposed to be. It was nowhere – not to the east, or to the west. There were no clues where it was either.

Grandpa thought of it first. He said, "I see the tops of trees broken along the shore to the east. The wind must have been strong here last night."

Boone could see Grandpa was right.

It was Pastor Andrew who solved the problem. "My guess is the wind picked up the boat and blew it somewhere. It may be partly submerged along the shore."

Boone was beginning to feel disappointed, it looked like the fishing trip on Loon would not happen. He walked a few more steps when he heard Pastor Andrew say words that brought joy to Boone's fisherman heart. "I'll go ask the landowner if we can borrow his boat, the one next to where our boat was. We have to search for the boat in the water...and we can do a little fishing besides."

"Saved, saved! Thank you, God!" Boone repeated to himself as he walked back to the pickup.

He and Grandpa began to take the fishing gear out of Pastor Andrew's pickup. The men were certain the land owner would say 'yes' to borrowing his boat. He man was known for his generosity. And they guessed right. Within minutes, Pastor Andrew had returned with good news. They could borrow the man's boat to search for their lost boat. They could also spend some time fishing.

Boone knew how relief felt just then. It was a good feeling. Boone decided relief felt better than getting something you really wanted badly for Christmas. Relief was better than a gift, relief removed unhappiness.

Boone did not know then that this fishing trip would produce a very unexpected surprise. The surprise involved a fish and the little boat. Boone was only thinking of getting on the water as they quickly moved things into the neighbor's boat.

Chapter 16

A Surprising Fish

"How great is your goodness, which you have stored up for those
who fear you, which you bestow in the sight of men on
those who take refuge in you."
— Psalm 31:19

At first, Boone was dissatisfied with boat hunting. He wanted to fish. Then the mystery grabbed his attention. Where was that little boat? They had walked the shoreline and all they got was wet feet from the dew on the grass. Where was the boat?

Boone's attention shifted quickly to boat hunting. But within minutes, the three occupants of the borrowed boat had given up hope of finding the boat partly submerged in the water. They went east along the shore, then turned and slowly moved west at the edge of the bulrushes. They looked in every place an opening in the rushes might suggest a partially submerged boat. There was no sign.

Boone heard Pastor Andrew sigh. Then these words floated to the front of the boat where Boone was puzzling over where their little fishing boat could be. "We should stop hunting and get to fishing, don't you think, Boone?"

At those words, Boone's head snapped up and he turned quickly back to Pastor Andrew. For a moment he just looked at Grandpa and Pastor Andrew.

He saw them reaching for their fishing rods. Boone found his voice, "Yes sir! Let's fish!"

Boone quickly forgot they were searching for their lost boat. His white spinner bait with the two silver flashers hit the water just after he saw Grandpa's bait splash down.

Fishing was always good, Boone thought, as the three of them worked their way to the west along the shore. Boone had already learned Pastor Andrew's fishing pattern for Loon Lake: stop at the fallen tree first. There was almost 20 feet of water just off the end of the tree, and with it, a good drop off that held fish.

Then he would troll slowly to the west, into the shallow bay to the north, then around the shore of the middle point on the north shore of Loon. That little bay often produced a fish, either a bass or northern. But today there were no fish at the tree or in the bay.

By the time Boone heard Pastor Andrew say, "Boone, drop the anchor any time you are ready," Boone still had not caught a fish and neither had Grandpa nor Pastor Andrew.

As he lowered the anchor, Boone remembered it was heavy and the chain was rough. But he got the anchor down and the boat secured without any loud clanks or clunks. The boat now rocked over the middle point of Loon Lake. Boone looked back toward the fallen tree before he made his first cast.

There will be fish here, he thought to himself confidently, and he threw the spinner bait to the east in the direction of the tree. Boone began his favorite spinner bait retrieve chant, "crank, twitch, sink...crank, twitch, sink."

He was on the word "sink" when the fish hit. Boone felt a downward pull, he knew it wasn't the lure sinking. Boone raised his rod tip quickly pulling up and back at once. *Good hookset,* he thought to himself, then out loud Boone softly said the words, "Fish on."

Then the fish shook its head and dove. *It's making a run to escape me,* Boone thought to himself. *You aren't getting away fish, I got you!*

The fish tired quickly after that. In a few more moments, Grandpa had the net under a fish that measured 15.5 inches. This one went in the cooler in front of Boone's feet.

"Just over two pounds, Grandpa," Boone said. "It will be delicious."

Boone's mouth began to water as he thought of a meal of fish again, soon. Before Boone made the next cast, he checked his knot and the line above the leader. His dad had taught him to do this. Sometimes the knot loosened and there were things that could fray the line and weaken it. It could mean the difference between a fish caught and a fish lost.

Then Boone heard the words he liked to hear most while in the boat: "Fish on!"

Boone turned to see Pastor Andrew's rod with a great bend in it. Since Pastor Andrew always fished for northern pike, Boone's first guess was right. Again, Grandpa had the net out. It took a few minutes. The fish made more than one run. Pastor Andrew gave no clue about the size of the fish. But Grandpa said, "I think this one is a good one."

All Boone could think of was, "Big."

And big it was! Grandpa had to turn the net to get the whole fish in, yet Boone could see the tail hanging over the edge.

Grandpa said two words fast: "Coming in!"

Then, as Boone watched with his mouth open, Grandpa swung the net into the boat between Pastor Andrew's seat and his. The noise was immediate. The big fish began to flop and twist. Boone stood in a crouch just high enough to see and watched as it rolled, twisting itself into the net.

"That's a mess," Boone thought.

He saw Grandpa reach down to grab the fish behind its gills. Between Grandpa and Pastor Andrew, the tangle disappeared and the big northern was stretched out and measured. Boone was almost ready to blurt out, "How long?"

Then he heard Pastor Andrew say, "36 inches, Boone, how much might it weigh?"

Boone looked into his tackle bag and took out the weight chart. He found 36 inches would equal nearly a 10-pound fish.

"Nine pounds 10 ounces, Pastor," Boone called softly to the back of the boat. Boone was shocked by what he heard next.

"This big one goes back in the lake. It's likely a female. She'll be the mother of many more northern in Loon if we release her."

With wide eyes, Boone continued to watch as Pastor Andrew carefully swung the fish over the side. He lowered it into the water and held it by the tail with its head down. Soon Boone could see the head of the fish wag from side to side as it attempted to free itself. Then Pastor Andrew let go. Slowly, the big fish swam downward and disappeared. Boone remembered the water was nearly 20 feet deep at this spot, just like at the fallen tree. The fish had plenty of water to make recovery to full strength.

What surprised Boone the most in those next moments was what Pastor Andrew said from the back of the borrowed boat.

"We should pull anchor now, Boone. It's time we moved on."

Boone didn't say what he was thinking. Instead, he answered with, "OK, Pastor Andrew...coming up!"

While he pulled the heavy claw anchor up, Boone thought to himself, *Why can't we stay here? Maybe there is another big fish?*

It seemed like Grandpa was reading his mind when he spoke. "Boone, that big fish thrashed around below the boat quite a bit. The other fish have moved off for a bit. We'll do better if we move on."

Boone had heard Pastor Andrew and Grandpa talking about prophets in the Bible on the drive to the lake. "If what is said comes to be, it is a good signal that person is a prophet," Pastor Andrew spoke with confidence.

Boone knew he did not understand everything about prophets, but a few moments later Boone heard the words he liked to hear most in the boat come again, this time from Grandpa's mouth.

"Fish on!"

Before he could catch himself, Boone blurted out, "Grandpa! You are a prophet!"

As the last syllable of the word "prophet" came from Boone's mouth, he felt shame. Had he spoken something to offend his Grandpa?

Almost as quickly, Boone heard laughter coming from the back of the boat. It was Pastor Andrew. "Right Boone, your Grandpa is a prophet...he's hooked a fish to prove it."

Boone quickly looked at Grandpa, who had a broad smile on his face.

As he fought to reel the fish in, he added, "Well, Boone, call me a fish prophet, not a Bible prophet."

Thinking about Grandpa's words, Boone decided on the location of his next cast. He would toss the white spinner bait toward the patch of lily pads along the shore.

He heard Grandpa's voice, "Boone, drop this one in the cooler with your bass, this one is just over 15 inches...it might be a bit more than a pound and a half."

With the fish safely in the cooler, Boone lined up for the cast to the patch of lily pads. Pastor Andrew had slowed the boat down, which meant Boone had more time with the retrieve on this cast.

Crank, twitch, sink.... Silently, Boone began his retrieve chant. This time he never got to "crank." Instead of the lure sinking rapidly, the entire rod and reel began to slip from his hands. Instinctively, Boone set the hook. The rod bent in a dangerous arc toward the side of the boat. Boone knew...this fish was BIG. It was only a semi-grunt, but he got it said, "Fish on!"

Then the fish shook its head. Boone thought the rod and reel would actually come out of his hands. Quickly, he released some tension on the drag, which was already ratcheting out as fast as tension would allow. Boone watched as the line sliced back to the lily pads.

"Oh, no, big fish, you aren't going back in there!" Boone said through clenched teeth.

Grandpa and Pastor Andrew chimed in together, "Hang on Boone!"

It seemed that time stood still and that hours went by, but just under five minutes later Grandpa slid the net under the bulky largemouth bass. This time he swung it to the floor of the boat behind Boone.

For a brief moment, all Boone could do was stare. It was easily the largest bass Boone had ever seen. Words did not come and Boone was unusually quiet. The silence was broken when the bass flopped loudly on the bottom of the boat. It thumped. Boone could feel it in his seat.

Grandpa broke the silence. "Well, Boone my boy, are we going to measure it?"

Boone felt himself blink. Then the words came, "Wow, wow, what a fish! Pastor Andrew can you see?

Boone glanced up. Yes, Pastor Andrew was on his knees looking past Grandpa's shoulder. Boone lay the tape on the nose of the fish, and Grandpa took it and squeezed the tail at the end.

"Boone! This fish is 23 inches long!"

Boone heard the excitement in his grandfather's voice. He knew what came next.

"Grandpa and Pastor Andrew, this big fish goes back to the lake right now."

Boone bent down and with his thumb and forefinger, lifted the biggest largemouth bass he had ever seen over the side of the boat. He grabbed its tail with his other hand and released his grip on the mouth of the bass. As the fish touched the water it gave a furious head shake. Boone lost his grip and watched in awe as the bass quickly returned to where it had come.

"That fish must have been over 7 pounds!" Boone said softly. Then he moaned out loud.

Grandpa was immediately worried. "Boone! What happened?"

Boone's answer came quickly. "We never took a picture. Grandpa, there's no picture! OH, boy, OH, boy!"

Then Pastor Andrew spoke up. All he said was, "Boone, look!" Pastor Andrew was holding up his cell phone. There on the screen was a picture of Boone and his grandfather with the tape on the fish. Boone could tell it was possible to read what the tape said on the picture. Boone was overcome.

"YAHOO!" he shouted.

As he put his phone away, Pastor Andrew softly said, "It's time to head back, isn't it?"

It was. The three fishermen began the short journey back to the landing. In a few minutes everything was loaded and the borrowed boat placed back where they had taken it from.

Boone could not contain himself. "Pastor Andrew, "We need another boat, don't we?" He watched as Pastor Andrew simply nodded.

As Pastor Andrew was driving down the drive of the neighbor, Boone looked out the side window of Pastor Andrew's pickup. His eyes moved to the little point of trees about two football fields east of the boat landing. Something was in the tall grass. Boone blinked. It was Pastor Andrew's little boat!

"Wait! Stop, Pastor Andrew, I see the boat on our left! It's by that point of trees along the shore!"

It did not take long for the three of them to arrive at the spot of ground where the boat lay. Boone's thought on the way was, *Yes, we can use it again when we haul it back to the landing!*

Then he saw the boat up close.

The transom, or back of the boat, was torn and damaged.

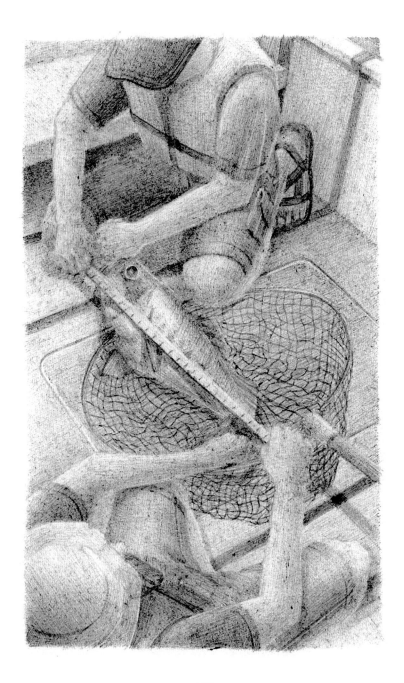

In fact, the right side of the back was ripped. As his eyes moved toward the front, he could see the entire center of the boat was pushed up against the middle seat.

"We won't be using this again," he heard Pastor Andrew say. "We'll leave it here today. I'll come back next week and haul it away."

Boone turned away with a sad look on his face. As he began walking back to the pickup, he felt a hand on his shoulder.

"Young man, I agree...we are getting another boat," said Pastor Andrew.

Chapter 17

"Power Checks" for Life

"I lift up my eyes to the hills—where does my help come from?
My help comes from the LORD, the Maker of heaven and earth.
— Psalm 121:1-2

Then it was over.

One day Boone realized the perfect relaxed days of summer were nearly over. A small wave of sadness came over him. Boone's summer had been better than expected. He would be ready for school to begin, but not until it was time. The sadness evaporated when he began to think of the changing leaves, the coolness of fall air and the coming migration. He knew "hard" water fishing would follow.

He had come to find peace and joy in "Power Checks." He had discovered how important time outside was for him. He was a different Boone. He had learned how the beauty God had put into every created thing calmed his heart down to his soul. Time outside softened the worries he had, made them seem less important. He found it easier to listen to his parents and much easier to speak to them with respect. Life in Boone's home had become more peaceful. Boone knew it was his behavior that destroyed the peace before. But the upset Boone showed up less and less, almost never. Boone knew he could not respect his parents, or control his tongue on his own. He needed help, much more than he could generate himself. Only God could give the strength he needed.

He had begun reading his Bible after his parents began "Power Checks" for him. Just a few days before school began, Boone read Psalm 121. At first, he did not see the connection to his life. He had been doing well. "Power Checks" were working, even though it had been a while since the last one. He made a mental note to sit on the family deck before sunset that evening and watch. But as he thought again about Psalm 121, he realized the words of the Psalm were absolutely for him.

Boone sat in the chair at his desk and wrote a prayer to God. He asked God to help him. He knew Psalm 121 spoke too of spending time in creation doing "Power Checks." Boone called it, *"The Hills."*

The Hills

Help!

Trouble has come!

Physical, emotional, spiritual...

in good times, one trouble at a time.

In bad, all three.

I worry, I'm unhappy, afraid.

Life is often hard.

Help! It's urgent. I can't wait for you God.

I'll do this myself. Sometimes I try.

When will I learn? Self-help never lasts. It's full of human error.

Help! Where does my help come from?

My help comes from the Lord!

He never slumbers, He does not sleep.

He watches over me...He helps me-forever.

Help me God. I can't do it myself.

Lift my eyes to the hills, that I may see you are my perfect Help.

"I lift up my eyes to the hills-where does my help come from?
My help comes from the Lord, the Maker of heaven and earth."
— Psalm 121:1-2

Epilogue:
For Parents and the Boones
Who Read this book...

This book is not based on fictional experiences. Most of them really happened in our family. The common feature in each chapter is the time Boone spent outside, and how being outside softens and brings peace to human hearts. I have personally experienced this and witnessed it occur in children as a teacher and grandfather.

Time outside should be considered a parenting strategy for every family. Boy or girl, children need time outside to balance the expectations, stressors and problems that come with growing up. Equally, adults benefit from time outside for the same reasons. Stress is reduced and problems that seem large indoors melt away, becoming manageable. Consider the benefit to the relationship with your child when the two of you spend time outside together. Consider stepping away from your family screens to the infinite big screen of nature.

Whether or not you have expressed it yet, you soon will...you are thinking, *I can't spend time outside with my child. I don't know anything about nature.* Good news, you don't need to know. Accompany your child outside and search for the divine nature and power of God together. When you go, there are some general things you may do together. Relax – you do not need to be an expert or even know anything about nature. Make discoveries with your child.

How to do "Power Checks" with your child:

Materials (keep this list short – your focus is nature)

1. A **journal** or two – lined or unlined. If you child cannot write, you do the writing – keep it simple. If they have learned to write, help them with words or ideas. Allow older children to write on their own while you write in yours. When you come inside before the day ends, share together.

2. A simple **thermometer** – use it to record temperatures of things: air, sky conditions, soil and water temperatures. Add a bit of science to your time outside.

3. **Pencils** work better in cold temperatures than pens. Consider colored pencils for sketches.

4. A **magnifying glass** – after you've been going out on nature walks a few times, take along a simple hand magnifying lens. Small things of the earth become exquisite when magnified.

What to do while outside together – "Power Checks"

1. **Walk without talking.** Give your walks immediate credibility. Call them *expeditions*. An expedition is *a journey with a purpose*. Listen and watch. Lean against a tree and continue to watch and listen. Consider standing, or better yet, sitting on the ground to watch and listen. Keep the first walk short. When back inside, pick up the journal, make a list together of what you saw and heard...remember God's power and divine nature!

2. **Lay on the ground.** After a few walks (expeditions) and a few sits on the ground, you and your child or children will be ready for the next delight – a *lay back*. Sit down and then lay down on the ground. Start with mowed grass and graduate to wilder places. Watch clouds if there are any. Name them if you wish. With no clouds, ask your outside partners to watch for birds. Spend time with your eyes closed just listening. Leave the journals inside yet, journal when you return. Write about what everyone saw and heard, with a focus on how they felt.

3. **Touch things, smell stuff.** With a few more walks outside, begin to invite your nature partners to touch and smell things you see. Of course, do neither if you are not sure it may be harmful. Things like tree leaves, tree trunks are generally safe. Begin to invite your partners to smell the earth beneath you, touch water nearby, smell flowers. The intent of this is to engage more senses. Always do this safely. When in doubt, don't.

4. **Look for signs of animals** living near you. The more time you and your nature partners spend outside, the more you will notice things. Begin to look for tracks, feathers, bits of fur. Nests are always interesting to beginning naturalists. Remind your hiking companions that the less talking you do on your hikes, the better chance you have to see wildlife. Tracks are a wonderful way to read the "story" of animal behavior in your area. Remember, you don't need to know what animal made them. At some point you may decide a track guide would be a good investment. You may want to identify what animal left the tracks. You may want to begin to carry your journals with you now.

5. **Sit and Watch.** This one will become your favorite – it is number five on the list for a reason. Give yourself and your nature companions time to gain experience outside watching, listening and thinking first. With experience, you will be prepared to enjoy this much more.

   For your first Sit and Watch, choose a familiar place you have already been to on one of your hikes. One criterion to follow in selecting your location is pick one with a minimum of human sounds. Traffic noise and sounds from human activity should be at a minimum at this place. Sit together the first time.

   One primary feature about a Sit and Watch is the absolute silence of those who sit and watch. Why? To allow the natural world around you to function as normally as possible in your presence. Think of the ripples that occur in a pond when a small stone is tossed in. For a Sit and Watch, wait in silence until the ripples of your presence have died away to actually see what happens with wildlife in this place.

Once you have done one together, you can place your nature explorers in their own spots. Choose places where you are separated but can see each other. When you have done this, take your nature explorers to a wilder place near your home such as a park, a wildlife refuge or a place in the country you have permission to visit. Sitting and watching in a wilder place when you have experienced it in your neighborhood will make lasting memories. Be sure to bring journals for these!

Consider Discovery Hikes:

Once your exploring team has experiences with the things in the list above, provide them with a variation. A *discovery hike* is a walk to *discover* what is happening in your neighborhood. Bring along the thermometer and the magnifying glass. Look for things that have changed since your last hike. Bring the journals along to make sketches, and record things like the temperature and things you witness.

In all of your "expeditions" search for the power and divinity of God. You will find it. Read Romans 1:20 with your explorers.

Author's Notes & Resources

Carson, Rachel. "Help Your Child to Wonder." *Women's Home Companion Magazine*. July, 1956. https://rachelcarsoncouncil.org/wp-content/uploads/2019/08/whc_rc_sow_web.pdf

Carson, Rachel. (Introduction: Lear, Linda). *The Sense of Wonder*. Harper Perennial. 2017. ISBN: 006757520X

Rachel Carson has been my mentor. We never met, but her *Help Your Child to Wonder* has given me many ideas as a teacher using nature for a classroom. The sense of wonder is a major part of discovering the beauty and joy to be found in nature. Get your own copy, read it again and again. You will discover something each time.

The Compass to Nature. United States Fish and Wildlife Service (USFWS). 2017.
https://www.fws.gov/uploadedFiles/Compass%20to%20Nature%20FINAL%20low%20resolution.pdf

The Compass to Nature is the product of personal experience. It developed from experiences gained as a teacher in the Fergus Falls Public Schools Prairie Science Class and as an Instructional Systems Specialist for the USFWS. *The Compass to Nature* is what you use when your goal is to connect adults and children to nature. It is easy to read and understand. Type in the link in your browser – it's free for you to use!

Murie, Olaus J. *A Field Guide to Animal Tracks*. Houghton Mifflin. 1954. ISBN: 0105101079

This is an excellent book on tracks. Whether you are a kid or an adult, learning to identify tracks allows you to understand what animals frequent the area where you live without seeing them. It is a fact – it is often difficult to see the animal, but it is quite easy to find its tracks. A tracks guide will add to your understanding of nature.

Kavanagh, James. *The Night Sky: A Folding Pocket Guide to the Moon, Stars, Planets and Celestial Events*. Waterford Press. 2017. ISBN: 162005280

The night sky is a guaranteed event to reveal the power and divine nature of God. I suggest a simple pocket guide to begin a study of the night sky. Begin, then spend the rest of life, at various times gazing into the heavens. Summer is a great time to begin. The mild evening temperatures make being outside comfortable. If you live in a city or town, remember street lights dimmish the view of stars…but start at home anyway. Later, be sure to plan a trip to a place where there are no street lights. You and your night sky partners will be amazed at the difference! Make night sky viewing a priority for you and your family.

Printable map of Northern Circumpolar Constellations:
https://acs.sharpschool.net/UserFiles/Servers/
Server_1282167/File/Staff%20Documents/Varsogea%20
Leslie/Pacing%20Documents/Fifth%20Grade/Fifth%20
Grade%20Science/Solar%20System/Circumpolar%20Star%20
Map%20Resource.pdf

Printable map of Southern Circumpolar Constellations:
https://www.constellation-guide.com/constellation-map/
circumpolar-constellations/

Teach yourself the circumpolar constellations. These constellations are visible whenever the sun is below the horizon in the north. Need a reason to learn them? Read Psalm 19:1-4.

Tekeila, Stan, *Birds of Minnesota.* Adventure Publications. 2004. ISBN:1591930375

Stan Tekeila has produced field guides for almost every topic in nature. From birds to trees, flowers to insects, Mr. Tekeila has produced well-organized field guides. Every guide has identifying photos of every subject – most were taken by Mr. Tekeila. I highly recommend them to you. In addition, these books are easy on your budget! As you seek a field guide for some subject in nature, easy for child and adult, begin with Mr. Tekeila.

The Holy Bible.

The Bible is a major book to read as you seek to understand how nature works. It is the main source of teaching for every person who desires to change behavior like Boone. Return to the Contents page for the list of Scriptures used in each chapter of the book. Then search the Bible for other passages God has placed there for our instruction. My prayer for you is for the book about Boone to lead you to the book written by God – the Bible.

About the Author

David Ellis

They say if you grow up on a farm you have "dirt" under your fingernails the rest of your life. You cannot see the dirt; my fingernails are clean. But the life of a farm boy, the life lived in the country, continues to be a key part of my life here on earth. My mother taught me the names of birds, plants and animals. With her I watched thunder clouds form in the west. The example of my father, the farmer always connected with creation through crops, livestock and daily farm life, instilled a love of creation in me that exists to this day.

During a career of more than 40 years as an educator, an elementary teacher and an Instructional Systems Specialist (teacher) for the United States Fish and Wildlife Service, I took children and adults outside whenever it was possible. Seeing the impact of nature on the hearts of humans blesses me greatly. Time outside *does* make a difference in the life of every human being.

Now a grandpa myself, my desire is to connect our grandchildren whenever possible to the beauty, mystery and wonder found in creation. It is my sincere belief that every human can see God in creation, that in creation the human soul finds comfort, peace and refreshment. In creation every human can "see" God.

Now retired, I find more time to do things with my wife, and our family. I have more time to spend outside. Besides composing this book about Boone, my days are filled with taking photos and writing about all things in creation. You can see both photos and text about nature at my blog:

creatorwords.com

About the Illustrator

Nate Christenson

Nate Christenson grew up in China with his parents and two brothers in a city of over eight million people. But even though nature could be sparse, he grew to love the outdoors — especially the times when he could get away into the surrounding mountains.

He started to develop the eye of an artist when he began to read chapter books and discovered that drawing the characters was something that he finally could do better than his older brother. Yet the initial competitive motivation quickly turned into a self-driven pursuit of art, which would eventually lead him to study drawing and painting at the Minneapolis College of Art and Design, and begin a career with his God-given creative abilities.

Nate now lives and works in the mountains of Ecuador with his wife, Britta, and two Maine Coon cats, Bagheera and Baloo.